VIA FOLIOS 114

What the Critics Said About Mark Ciabattari's *Dreams of an Imaginary New Yorker Named Rizzoli*

"A collection of funny frightening pieces dealing with the extraordinary life of an everyman called Rizzoli in a really mad, mad world."

—*Associated Press*

"Rizzoli is an anxious anti-hero ... an urban everyman. [His] ... funny, satirical, vignette-like dreams [show] the influence of media on our perceptions [and] point to our mediated lives, to commercials that advertise instant love as ardent strangers pursue each other with flowers." — *The New York Times Book Review*

 "...part Beckett, part Woody Allen..." — *Kirkus Reviews*

"An original, humorous fantasy... of sometimes frightful beauty...."

—*Il Giorno* (Milan)

"Ciabattari's art and wit are everywhere present in his character's dazzled and frazzled psyche..." — *Booklist*

"Ciabattari has... combined the metropolitan terror of Kafka with the...slapstick and rhythm associated with fine cinematic montage. Postmodern, with the nervous vitality central to the literary myth of New York." — *Il Messaggero* (Rome)

"Ciabattari... brims with brio in this fanciful, cannily humorous look at the jungles of darkest Manhattan."

–*Publishers Weekly*

"This surreal fantasy returns you to Melville, with Rizzoli the descendent of the strange Bartleby, a personage who takes refuge in the dream." –*La Stampa* (Turin)

"Rizzoli fights the odds in this crazy city, armed with nothing but a shield of dreams." — *Newsday*

Praise for Mark Ciabattari's *The Literal Truth*

"With unerring irony, Ciabattari paints a shimmering, disorienting world in which the lines between dreams and reality are systematically skewed... Set against the vibrant backdrop of New York City and the Hamptons, Rizzoli's chaotic life seems to be a natural extension of the city and human consciousness."

— Publishers Weekly

"A delightfully improbable blending of Borges and Woody Allen."

— Booklist

"Ciabattari's Chaplin-esque walker in the city returns in a series of surreal, episodic and intellectually playful cinematic dreamscapes that veer from wish fulfillment to nightmare.... A paean to the special "city grace" that prevails amid chaos, Ciabattari's novel is a delightful postmodern romp, more Calvino than Kafka."

— Kirkus Reviews

"With deft twists of prose, Ciabattari evokes a life that is a dream within a dream...
Rizzoli stands with us, outside his own inside joke. His brief dreams have the aura of certain Zen koans, pushing us to wonder, 'I think I get it ... do I get it?' Ciabattari declines the easy answer."

— The Washington Post

From Fred Gardaphé's Introduction to Ciabattari's *Clay Creatures*

"... it is writers like Ciabattari who remind us only by imagining can we transcend where we are and go to places we have never been. This is progress. This is Ciabattari."

— Fred Gardaphé

Preludes to History

Preludes to History

The Head, The Satyr And The Mermaid

Mark Ciabattari

BORDIGHERA PRESS

Library of Congress Control Number: 2015937923

Printed in the United States.

Published by
BORDIGHERA PRESS
John D. Calandra Italian American Institute
25 West 43rd Street, 17th Floor
New York, NY 10036

VIA FOLIOS 114
ISBN 978-1-59954-096-2

TABLE OF CONTENTS

The Head

Rome: 1938-1944

"History is a nightmare from which I am trying to awake."

— *James Joyce*

Part I

(1)

At midnight beginning the day of 15 January 1938, 22-year-old Vico Matteo Rizzoli stopped working for a moment shortly into his first shift as the museum janitor in the Criminology Museum in Rome. Leaning on his broom, for a moment, at a slight tilt due to a lame leg, he thought about these past twelve hours. *I will never forget. Never.*

He would always remember coming by train, arriving in the morning a stranger in Rome; and the State hiring him by noon for this, his first real job; including the benefits of lodging in the museum's basement room with meals. Six hours ago, a simple pasta dinner appeared, hot. Now, he had only ten hours left on his shift. *This past half day I'll never forget.*

By now most good Romans must be asleep, Rizzoli thought. Faint yellow lights cast a slight glare on the dark wood of this upper floor where he swept, his broom's straws going back, forth. Its whisking resounded in this cavernous exhibit space, as he moved about the free standing, glass-fronted cases displaying some of Italy's past most notorious criminals and those in the state who brought them to justice.

Smiling, he thought of the emphasis: all criminals come to justice, especially under the Fascists. No criminal escapes the all-seeing watch of this State. His smile widened as he calculated the many who had, in fact, escaped forever the clutches of the state.

Italy's Number One Criminal. Il Duce! Someone shouted. Someone shouted. Did someone from my past blurt that out? he wondered, not recognizing it as one of his own usual mind voices. *So forceful, I came close to shouting it out.*

Since beginning his shift at midnight he had looked at some of the unusual exhibits, reading bits about the lurid law-breaking and once hunted outlaws from the past. In the dimly lit museum surrounded by night darkness, he had the eerie feel of being outside the furthest borders of society. He sensed his work would soon settle into a comfortable routine and he'd come to his own peace with these ghostly outcasts.

He came to the end of one row of display cases and, looking up, saw a headline honoring Italy's current world-renowned crime fighter, the criminologist, Cesare Lombroso. Rizzoli was wildly surprised. He had assumed the displays did not include living persons. Wrong. Under glass right here were text and illustrations chronicling the achievements of this famed criminologist. Rizzoli had heard about Lombroso since he was a boy in his village in Liguria north of Genoa.

Lombroso! The man who can predict if any child or adult will or will not be a future criminal! Rizzoli's mama used the word "Lombroso" to scare Rizzoli when he did something bad, adding a threat: "You will become a criminal!"

In the dim light and rush to finish this night's work Rizzoli squinted and read the text hurriedly, jumping ahead to passages that caught his attention. "Lombroso's sterling reputation now in the 1920s and 1930s comes when research into genetic social deviation is held in the highest regard — a time devoted by geneticists to improving select races and eliminating their unfit."

He skipped, read more, glanced ahead until he stopped at a sheet reading, "Lombroso's Most Famous Experiment." "Italy's world famous criminologist Dr. Cesare Lombroso, in 1910, with the aim of proving criminal traits were inherited, with the approval of the State, had the head of the anarchist Giovanni Passannante severed for experimental studies on a skull with a brain still alive..." (*Alive!*)

The State. THE STATE! Severed it? No, approved. Approved. So, now where is Passanante's head, made bodiless in 1910...? And a live head conceived how? So it seems the body buried in the southern Basilicata region in 1910, now rotted in the ground some 28 years ago, had been headless. Head lopped off then – it all had to have been hush, hush with the Church surely in on this matter, then likely advising the State that the Criminal Passannante had no immortal soul. Ever.

Switching to the second background sheet, he read on "The Criminal: Giovanni Passannante, (1860-1910)". An anarchist, he died and was buried at age fifty in his native southern Italy. At a young age in 1878, this criminal nearly assassinated newly united Italy's Head of State, King Umberto I.

He skimmed the rest very fast, noting, "For this crime – what *anarchists then called Propaganda of the Deed – The State sentenced him ...*" (*The State?*) "...to death, then commuted this to a lifetime sentence, jailing him alone on the Isla of Elba and keeping him in isolation for nearly three decades. Near the end, Passannante went insane. He spent his last three years in a mainland asylum, seeing visions."

Standing there, Rizzoli had the odd feeling that someone was about. He completed his night's chores, finishing his shift, put his supplies away and started down the stairs to his room. It was ten a.m. *Food?* He hoped this morning that he'd see a dry roll or something left on his table, He was grateful to the mysterious someone who had left him his meager dinner the night before.

(2)

His work plan was on schedule. *Tomorrow night, after my second shift, I will have swept the entire exhibit floor. The rest of this week, I will mop the floors then polish the brass.*

Entering his tiny living space at 10:15 a.m. by his pocket watch, he looked at his small rough wooden table. *Who?* There on its bare top he saw his one plate with a piece of broken off bread and a bit of white cheese and a fruit glass of red wine. Still dressed in his work clothes—corduroy pants, collarless shirt, vest—he sat in his one chair. He laid his cloth cap aside on the table's rough wood. He ate and drank gratefully and thanked whomever the person was who had left this breakfast.

He cleared the table and cleaned the dishes under the cold-water spigot with the catch basin on the floor. Then he sat alone in his tiny basement room. He wanted to keep his mind from focusing on the Head.

A random thought suddenly struck him. *Maybe this is like a casual no-show job and that's all the big man was trying to get across upon hiring me.*

"Room and board, a paycheck, eh?" he said. "What more could you ask for? A public job with a title, 'State Custodian,' so you can earn the rewards, maybe?" Then, he'd laughed. Is that what he'd meant?

Even if it was, Rizzoli had honor and could not let down his uncle or his family back in the village in the foothills of the Alps in his beloved Liguria, the coastal province in the far North. So dim are these memories, now in the museum it seems my prior life in Liguria was always a fantasy and had never occurred.

His train from Genoa to Rome had roared into the great railroad station in the late morning the day before. Standing up in his passenger compartment, retrieving his single small, strapped suitcase from the overhead rack, he saw himself reflected in the window. He was tall, lean, and, in his Mama's words, oddly handsome, with dark wavy hair, a clean-shaven face, and brown eyes. He wore his one suit, dark, owned by his papa previously, and that his dear mama tailored to size, careful to make the pant leg shorter for his slightly lame leg.

He had an appointment with a high official set up by his Uncle Ettore, a powerful Roman judge appointed by Mussolini. Ettore met him at the train platform, gave him a quick onceover, and said, "Very fine. You are sure to make a good appearance. Good luck. I have business."

To get from the station to the appointment, he had walked the stone streets of Rome, a total newcomer. He had no memory of that part. Likely I was so worried about going astray from Ettore's directions and being late, I was too focused on the trees to see the forest. What's more here inside the museum, he found it difficult to recall personal details occurring outside these walls.

He paused, pondering this memory gap. *How strange. My first time seeing this eternal city and when I try to recall it, I draw a blank.* At about one-thirty, at the designated place, after a long patient wait, the important man, whose name he couldn't remember, came and said, "You are the one for the job."

How elated I was at that news I would be the night janitor at this new tourist attraction, the Museum of Criminology. Can you imagine a museum of the past great outlaws of Italy? And tonight at work he had eagerly seen some of those exhibits. "Remember," the important man had said. "You have a boss, but you'll likely never see him because he's all over doing the business of the Party."

"Thank you," Rizzoli said. He went the few blocks from the big man's office to the museum in a daze, reliving the hiring. A sheet of work duties would be left for him at regular intervals, the important man had explained. "The main thing is you will know to keep up the right appearance in the museum. Otherwise you're on your own. You work and live alone in the museum. Think of it as home."

Alone? Always before Rizzoli had been immersed in the village, family, generations of people. *Alone? Home? My head I have all to myself here.* "Do a little work, no one's going to bother your head," said the big man. "Your quarters are down in the basement, Room X4. Here's the ring of keys to it all. You'll need to try them out, find your supply closet and all. I'll see that your luggage arrives. To the museum from here is an easy walk. You've the time. Enjoy yourself. Good luck, I must go now."

"Thank you." Rizzoli went the few blocks to the museum in a daze, still stunned at being hired.

(3)

A few nights later as Rizzoli was in the middle of his mopping he realized his schedule and duties were becoming a routine. He was confident now of being able to do well at this job. He'd been slightly nervous at first at having never done a janitor's duties. A night shift of ten straight hours and sleeping in the day was also becoming familiar.

He was keenly aware of this being his first secure regular paying job. *Not bad, a state employee, starting at the lowest pay, but with free lodging and meals. I don't want to mess this up. Even if the big man who hired me was hinting I just have to do a little work every now and then, I'll do good work every shift.*

Coming to a corner of a wall at the end of a row of exhibits, he moved his bucket, put the mop in it and leaned back against a section of the adjoining wall. Rizzoli fell back surprised as the nondescript white wall's sections gave in, accordion-like, to reveal a separation between it and a second wall with the scant outline of a door. It had the tiniest of keyholes.

Startled, needing better light to check his ring of keys, he turned and walked backward, tilting to the side with each step of his lame right leg. (*This ring of keys, I must know by heart; no tiny key, no.*)

But, there it was, buried amidst the larger ones. He went back and tried the key several times with slightly different pressure and angle. The lock turned on the fourth try. He pushed in. Darkness. A light went on. In the middle of the room, right there, his eyes locked onto a horrifying sight.

Dead eyes, yellowed skin, hallowed mouth in a detached, preserved human head. The eyes stared at Rizzoli from inside a closed-off, sealed glass vitrine on a pedestal. Wanting his eyes to unlock, he could only stare on, terrified. *It's a Mussolini experiment for Futuristic Fascist Man. In a tank for a goldfish, only this one has ... a Fascist, if he is. Age forty?*

Vowing to show courage no matter what, Rizzoli swaggered forward for a closer view. Suddenly, he saw two thin wires with narrow clear tubes coming out of the straight, thin strands of reddish-gray hair, slicked to the back of the skull. Exiting from the head through tiny holes in the glass, the tubes went outside to a desk-top machine with levers and gauges.

It occurred then to him, this could be a *secret laboratory for developing a new type Fascist ... an informer? Set The Head in some secret place, let it soak up all talk, then retrieve it and give a meaningful storyline to all the confusing, contradictory aspects of the talkers.* The face had a look of strength from the underlying, chiseled bone structure. The nose was broad, mustache stringy, with traces of red. Looking up close at the (unseeing?) yellowed eyes, he saw that the irises were once blue.

The face's frozen expression was one of bemused contempt—*at me? No.* Rizzoli smiled and then confused, curled his lip at The Head. *You don't intimidate me,* he thought and with added bravado, *So, I lose my job for seeing The State's new*

Head of Intelligence. So WHAT? No, wait I don't want to lose my job.

Now he glanced around the room; on a single shelf, waist high, he saw a small stack of papers; he took it down. One sheet of information had what seemed to be a draft for a placard, as if this at one time was going to be opened as another exhibit but then a decision had been made against that.

He began reading; starting with the heading: "The Giovanni Passannante Experiments (1910 into 1930s)." Suddenly, he thought he heard a noise outside (*I forgot to fold back the wall!*). He read rapidly by glances: "...Electrical Wires, Brain Sockets, Breathing Tube, Blood Circulator and Sound Transmitter .As used by Lombroso, these originals aimed to probe Passannante's brain for leftover memory pool voices (none were found) or, for brain wave static (evidence did show these) persisting long after the heart ceases to beat...."

He skipped ahead: "...the head you see is still attached with the full array, recently inserted, of functioning replicas of devices used in the experiment." Astonished by all this, he read further. The glass cube "...is a vitrine with a near perfect vacuum inside to preserve the head's features. The clear tubes going from outside the cube inside it and on into the skull pump oxygen, blood and other fluids to keep the brain alive for any possible future experiments... " (*Alive? In a manner of speaking only.*) So this head had been switched from being an old anarchist into *now being a Fascist informer! Yes!*

Why else keep this "live" head so well maintained, yet hidden away as an invisible agent of the Fascist state? *Otherwise, why were the Head's life-giving mechanisms so well main-*

tained? What if the Head aided in negating some clear and present danger to Il Duce and his Fascists?

He carefully put back the stack of papers, left the room, carefully closed it up with the tiny key, put the door section in place and resumed his work.

Refusing to give any more thought to this, he went on with his mopping and stopped just before ten a.m. He cleaned and stored his materials and went to his room, tired after another ten hours.

(4)

The next day, to get his mind off his bizarre discoveries, Rizzoli decided to go to the museum's café-bar on the street level. He casually changed into his one suit and left his room. He went down the hallway and up the stairs to the first floor, turning one corner, then another. He suddenly came upon a large, thick one-way glass door with a crowd inside, all merrily mingling, standing, sitting, drinks in hands.

The Café! Unseen, out of hearing range, Rizzoli looked on, hidden by the glass and studied the scene's silent pandemonium. Inside, all were like mimes, talking, laughing, gesturing and drinking. The varied social mix was dazzling; high- and low-born, army officers, peasants, black shirts, workers with tiny red flags in their lapels, judges, lawyers, clerks, priests, and even a bishop or a cardinal. Rizzoli had never imagined so many classes gathering socially. What were they saying?

Stepping unnoticed through the secret glass door, Rizzoli instantly heard a wave of loud sounds; talk, the clinking of glasses, laughter of all sorts, the hissing of the espresso machine. He began edging his way slowly through the thick crowd. A waiter gave him a free glass of red wine.

Suddenly, he was aware of overhearing a clash of many startling bits of random conversations. Persons revealed their most secret selves. *Like a collective confessional. Confidential. Not for the State's uses?* Not surprisingly, he heard much talk of current history. Some of it was meant for harmless public consumption, other comments revealed behind-the-scenes information full of complicated personal power struggles, betrayals, deceits.

Rizzoli started hearing bits of another conversation between an anarchist and two black-shirted Fascists.

"Mussolini is wary, yes, that some anarchist here in Italy will try to kill him," one of the Fascists said. "No one has so far, but it's a worry to him."

"Who knows," the anarchist said, "I, Giancarlo, could be the one to do the deed."

All laugh. "Yes, " answered the second Fascist. "And I wouldn't have a clue who to look for as the assassin. Your face, our conversations, everyone here will be a blank once I'm out the door. Outside no one has any memory of whatever happened inside the café."

What? Once out that door, Rizzoli thought, then, Bam! They say you will never know of time spent inside? *Does that mean that I, who don't leave this building, when in the café, will be able to remember patrons and their revealed secrets? Does it mean I will accumulate the people and their secrets as long as I live here and do not go out? That I could have access to the café's collective memory, and become deeply entangled in ongoing events?*

Strangely, in the café, I don't get the blind urge, as others seem to do, to reveal my own deep secrets. But I've never gone outside. How can I say what it would be like to come in fresh?

And this silent Head? He could be a futuristic informer who will soak up valuable café memories from my mind. I vow, now from this early January 1938 onward, I will leave the Head in his solitude. Maybe he's brain dead anyway.

(5)

With this vow to avoid the Head, Rizzoli went back to his room and changed into his work clothes. He discovered an unlabeled amber bottle of table wine left in his room. He didn't exactly know when or by whom, but he relished the wine as a reminder of his earlier life in the village.

Since age sixteen, he had worked doing seasonal and odd jobs. Images came to him of the terraced vineyards, and winding olive groves. He was never left wanting, even after he became slightly lame from an overturned donkey cart. He had always had work. This was especially so because employers had come to believe he could fix anything mechanical, especially any newfangled things.

Tired from the day's work, he laid his folded hands on the table and began thinking of his new job. *So now I'm an official employee of the State. The State! The State? Yet I don't know what The State is exactly and why IT stays even when rulers and governments pass on. It's not like The Sky, is it? There. There — always, no matter what?*

In Liguria, The State was no place other than Rome. Taxes, national police, rules and harsh laws – all came from there, the center. It was hated. It was powerful and could crush an individual. What of me? Its employee? What if I mess up? I'd be in real danger. But if I keep a low profile, IT won't know who I am. Or, even, if I am. It's so huge.

He decided to get some sleep. He lay down on the single narrow bed with the wrought iron bedstead. He slept until about six o'clock. When he woke up, his thoughts were racing. He suddenly recalled his dream of the anarchist and the scientist arm wrestling with their heads each under a guillotine, blades high up ready to drop, *on the loser, was it? Or, was it the winner?* He couldn't remember which. Meanwhile, a voice in the dream announced, "In the left-hand corner, the anarchist vows, 'Death to the State.' In the opposing corner, the scientist holds the belief, 'Nothing stands higher than the State.'"

As he lay there, he had a feeling that the way Lombroso (or, the restorers) had wired the Head had lacked the aesthetic sense that Rizzoli always had about the workings of new mechanical devices. He pictured how the boxed-in glass Head was hooked up to the outside "listening machine" with earphones. Tubes from the vitrine attached to the top of an outside metal box.

Wires going from its bottom connected to maximum survival devices for the Head, its supplies of blood and oxygen – these seemed well maintained (likely by the State), Rizzoli thought. The listening machine was linked to four wires— two coated colors and two more of different metals—Rizzoli felt these needed to be switched — the red with blue, and silver metal with bronze,

(6)

Coming out of the rest room, he heard, "Handsome, come over, have a seat." A woman's voice was calling to him. He turned around.

"You, yes. Come sit with us," said a society woman sitting with another blond woman and, a bishop? The women smiled. Instinctively, he smiled back. *Do they know me?* He went over, introduced himself and sat down. The sultry blond filled his glass full of wine and said, "I'm Lena."

"I'm Sophia."

"Bishop Insalati."

"So we were just arguing who were the better lovers — those strutting Fascists you now see all over like black flies or, the daring anti-fascists of the opposition. Of course, our bishop here prefers to molest little girls and boys, don't you?" The bishop smiled, yes, and smoothed the lap of his green satin robe. " I would take you to be one of the anti-fascists, "the blond said. "Am I right? The countess knows."

"Who's to say?" Rizzoli answered her.

"Never mind that," said the countess, "Isn't this café wonderful — in here for as long as you want, you can say whatever you want — curse the Fascists, tell a top state secret and still be a true Fascist in real life. Or be in the opposition and relieve the stress of hating Fascists silently by openly flirting with one of their women here in the café. Then, smile and chat with her Fascist lover, husband. Then go out, forget and be true again in real life."

"And never with any consequences," the other woman added. "You know, all revealed in the café is forgotten, is a blank once you go through that door back out into the streets of Rome."

"Why do you think Sophia there likes to come in here and make it in the one small back bedroom with some young peasant hunk, even though she's a countess in real life and could never be seen with the likes of you or a trollop like me? Who would know? Not even Sophia herself once out the door?"

Rizzoli looked at the secret back door again. "Ladies, I must excuse myself but, await my return soon another night," he said, getting up, determined to slip unseen through the back wall glass and get back to his room.

"Nooooo," Sophia said. Rizzoli smiled and winked.

As Rizzoli headed to the back door, a classy looking man in a black suit and fedora took him aside. "All we Fascists like you and me".... *He is talking to me?* "...like you and me, we need this release from the stress of being born the superior race and naturally having to tolerate our inferiors in our African colonies. Did you read the other day that Lombroso termed Italians a branch of the Aryan race? No surprise there."

Rizzoli smiled, and said, "I must get on. Sorry.

The Fedora Fascist asked if Rizzoli came often to the café. "Every now and then," Rizzoli answered purposely casual.

"Whenever you get the urge, huh, friend?"

Friend? Who is this? Rizzoli answered, "That's right."

"You know, I'm pleased all have to leave the building," said the Fascist.

"I'm glad, too, we all have to leave the building " Rizzoli lied,

" What if there was some poor character forced always to live in the museum, frequent the café, and never forget the growing burden of our public and secret sides," the Fascist continued. "Make a captive of history out of anyone, wouldn't it, friend?"

History's captive? Rizzoli had never heard that term.

"…wouldn't it, friend? Especially, if the person knew the direction of our history, could change it, tried and failed and then could only be a knowing victim of history's future on- slaught, huh?"

"That never occurred to me." Rizzoli needed to give some thought to this, especially the idea of the museum in- sider being a captive of ongoing hidden history spewed out by the café patrons.

"Excuse me, I need to be on my way now, friend," the Fascist said.

Rizzoli waited for him to leave. Then, he slowly worked his way to the secret glass back door. Glancing back to make sure the Fedora Fascist was not watching, Rizzoli slipped out into the hallway to go to his room, change and get to work. His watch said 11:15 p.m.

Rizzoli went down the hallway to his room, quickly changed clothes and went up the stairs to work.

(7)

I'll figure out what Lombroso tried and then I'll try a variety of ideas of my own about connecting the brain to the machine.

In the months ahead and on up to April 1938, Rizzoli kept up a search for an error in the brain-machine and made a comfortable routine of work, breakfast and a good sleep and going to the café bar in the late afternoon, coming back and changing clothes to start work at midnight.

His idea about the re-linking the wires he tried in varied ways but with no good result. He was out of ideas and slightly discouraged. In the café, Rizzoli overheard stunning state secrets and stories of the intimate flaws of leaders. He felt a personal complicity in knowing of these matters; for some he knew, he could be executed. Never meant for an ordinary man, these private revelations were only for the ears of an elite of Church and State. He worried about blundering and blurting out something, sometime.

One night in the room of the Head, Rizzoli experimented in a manner different than before. He opened the outside metal box and redid one electrical wire inside it to make a slightly different circuit from the phone device to "the brain probe sockets" still in Passannante's head. There, in the dead of night, he tried his latest way to make contact with the mind of the now 78 year-old-head of Passannante, twenty-eight years bodiless and without a heart.

"Are you there, Passannante?" he asked.

Silence.

"Is there someone can hear me?" *Nothing. BRAIN DEAD.*

"Is this the voice of the one from outside?" A coarse voice came from within the skull.

"What? WHA! WHA!" Rizzoli blathered. *Calm down*, he thought before answering." This voice is me. My name is Vico Matteo Rizzoli."

"They sent you? Are you one of us?"

"Who?" *Whose side is the Head on?*

"If you have to ask, you don't belong."

Ignoring that, Rizzoli said, "I'm the new night janitor here at the museum of criminals."

"I know that and your background. You, Rizzoli are the son of a schoolteacher and went two years to university. When he died, you and mama became part of her good peasant family in a village in Liguria. You did farm chores and fixed many things. Right?"

"Right. How could it be, you know this about me?"

Passannante went on, "You can write, but more important, you have savvy, intelligence, and common sense. You are both an intellectual and what I describe as one of the real people."

"So I'm a real person, me. For certain, what else?"

"But, am I, Briganti, who forms and converses with you only in my mind, real or not? Isn't that what you want to know? What if you are a character I constructed in this ongoing make believe story? No, you will say. I am of my own mind, eh?"

Before Rizzoli can answer, the Head rushed his words. (*Talks non-stop with himself, I bet, always making up a story to kill time*) "Maybe you will learn with time and maybe not. Depends on you, Frizzoli." (*Still a lunatic.*)

"Rizzoli, not Frizzoli."

"Rizzoli, that's what I said."

Head said "Frizzoli."

"Well, I do know some about you, too" answered Rizzoli. "What I read before says you were a young anarchist named Passannante who tried to knife to death the Italian King in 1878. Years jailed on the Island of Elba in isolation. Insane last few years. Died 1910, and soon after the scientist Lombroso severed your head and experimented on you in his lab.

"I am no longer that person—a short time after 1910, I became a different person."

A lunatic still, has to be. No harm in going along to find out more.

"You gave yourself a different name after that?"

"Not me, but 'they' began calling me, Briganti del Luca."

"Briganti the Light, eh? You know you are now positioned most unusually?"

"A head inside a fish tank, I am, in a closed, secret side room, in a criminal museum, in a small forgotten part of an official building with a ground level café-bar fronting a side street in Rome. A fish tank is a perfect headquarters for one to plot and lead what needs to be done in the hidden struggle for man's future."

What needs to be done? Rizzoli refrains from asking. *Don't make yourself appear in the dark here.* "Perfect, Briganti, yes," he said.

"Furthering this subject for the moment," The Head asked, "what is your aim in life?"

Rizzoli took a long deliberate pause. Silence. He decided to take the question seriously, *and remain true to myself.* "I want to lead a simple life but this is not easy when you're within the State. In short, I want to get through life and die without the State making me kill another human."

"That sentiment in itself I like — and besides, it gives you a perfect foil," said the Head.

"Foil? It's my real conviction. Sounded like you meant my cover."

"You said cover. I didn't say cover."

"Yet, you are an employee of The State," Rizzoli heard him say. "You serve Mussolini. How do you know this ruler won't make you kill?"

"I'm lame so I'm unqualified for his army."

"So, you're out, Rizzoli, but content to let the other young men of your generation do the killing in your stead for the glory of Il Duce who promises to make each a warrior in his modern Roman legions."

"I can't be responsible for those who want to be the new Romans of today."

"Fine. All I'm saying is that your young life seems to lack idealism — you know, responsibility for the betterment of all Humanity.

"Responsibility, *for all Humanity.* Me? A janitor? Think what you're saying."

"You do a good job of covering up, making yourself sound convincing. They made a good choice. You will work well."

"They! Who are they, Briganti?"

" Our movement has eyes and ears everywhere."

"They do? You don't say."

Then, wanting to draw this lunatic out, Rizzoli innocently asked in a kind voice, "If you will, could you answer a question for me, How were you able to suffer yet remain silent as Lombroso almost daily used electrical jolts to probe your mind? It was like a daily torture, no?"

" With all gone but my head, I only had will and a plan: inner exile, cunning and silence. The test was, never to let on to the scientists I was alive in here all that time. I somehow managed to do that. I also wanted to prevent future State leaders from finding a way to torture the dead into confessions."

"Bravo, you stood your ground."

"I did—with the help early on of a surprise reward—a visitation from a member of the village of truest humanity— real *paesani, verissimi paesani*. My saving vision, it was and my aim from that time on has become to remain true to my mind's idealism made real. The Little Italy, it is—and not the State. My vision exists—not up in some heavenly sky—but ongoing, here on earth, in a never discovered island village where humankind is at its best, living in peace and happiness."

"Hard for me to think this village can remain secret for the future. You did say secret, right?"

"I did," said Briganti. "Here's been the trick for centuries. Back in mythic times, the villagers learned how any potential intruders could be transformed from popes, priests, generals, bankers, nobles, soldiers into something productive or beautiful like trees, frogs, birds, strands of grain, a grape vine, a flower or a cold water spring."

Rizzoli is stunned at the imagination of the vision. *This is a vision though — seeing visions, wasn't it a sign of his insanity in 1910?*

"Briganti!! A village undiscovered to this day! In Italy! Briganti, you don't know what you've said — every inch of Italy has been tramped on for centuries — by all."

"Believe what you will. This village is primordial, pre-classical and comes down to our day. But, have it your way, Rizzoli. (*He laughed*). Village spies often frequent the café and come and give me information to interpret current history with the goal of keeping aggressors distant from our home."

The Head paused and his voice became grave. "These sources of mine chose you for a special reason — you and only you can change the path of current world history…"

"What! Me? Change world history? You've got the wrong person, not a unknown janitor…"

"However, in doing so, you will become an activating part in that history thereafter and be a captive of its evolving future."

"Interesting," Rizzoli said, having the clear idea Briganti was cuckoo. No answer from the Head.

Who knows if this village is just in this lopped-off head's mind? Who is he really? Son-of-a-bitch scares me. With that Rizzoli vowed to be wary upon returning again to this Room of the Head.

"Good night." he said. No answer. Rizzoli pulled the wires and hurriedly left the room, worried someone might discover him here without permission of an authority.

(8)

So all's forgotten for those who go outside but not for the likes of me who dwell within the building, Back in his room, an angry Rizzoli had devised a plan of escape. He would carry it out slowly, calmly and deliberately. Dressed in his nicest clothes, he left his room, then turned this way and that, left, down another unknown hallway, a path to escape, he hoped. He turned Left. Right.... Left. No door outside yet.

He began running and running. His heels clicking, then clattering, sounded a crescendo on the marble floor. Finally he stopped across from a bronze, wall plaque. He read: "Fascism reasserts the right of the State. The fascist idea of the State takes in everything. Outside of it no human or spiritual values can exist, much less have value. Il Duce Benito Mussolini. "

With that, he dropped to his knees, leaned against a white marble wall, exhausted and lost in this museum building maze. Does a labyrinth surround the café-bar? Weary, he slumped and dozed, sprawled flat on the floor.

Rizzoli awakened a short while later, body stiff from the cold hard marble. He rubbed his eyes and sat up. Recalling running and being lost in the maze of hallways, he sensed that the museum's street walls were like the bones of a skull.

The State or Head, one or the other, maybe, has me trapped inside this museum building, no way out of it, as I'm wound up in whatever my character's role is in history as understood by the Head's Mad Mind fashioning itself The Muse of History. Is that it?

Meanwhile, Rizzoli thought, cooperation is my best bet. He still believed there was a way out of his predicament. He got up off the floor, smoothed his suit, calmly chose a new route and again began walking the maze of hallways. Still lost but not panicked, he was confident of finding his room. His wristwatch read 2: 05. p.m. Ten hours still before work. He was relieved.

The café-bar! Slipping in through the back door, Rizzoli looked across the room to where all entered and exited: the impressive brass-handled door with frosted glass. After his eyes adjusted to the dim light inside, he saw the cafe was crowded with customers. He kept looking across them to the door outside to Rome. *The door!*

Rizzoli knifed through people until he was almost within arm's reach of the door.

"Excuse me, sir. I need to get by, please." He said.

Space opened.

"Thank you."

Reaching out, he clasped the handle of the magic door and discovered he could not turn it. He began straining and grunting, sure his face must be turning red.

"Here, let me give you a hand," a man said, easily turning the handle holding the door open with ease and grasping Rizzoli by the elbow. Pretending to be casual, smiling, Rizzoli strained, veins popped out on his neck and forehead.

His next crucial step outside, was it beyond him? "Come on, you. We people behind need out!" a voice behind ordered.

A barrier like a large invisible balloon stopped him. *Son of a bitch FASCIST STATE has me locked inside ITS building, trapped within ITS contradictions,* he thinks—but *IT better think again.* Rizzoli returned to the cafe, to the express relief of those impatient ones behind him.

(9)

Back in his room, overcome with emotion, he sat at his chair, head back and looked up at a crack on the ceiling for a long while. Glancing down, he saw a small fruit glass full of blood red wine with its dark amber bottle. *Had the kindly someone come in unseen and left it?* Either that or he had seen the wine at first, too, he thought, *just didn't note it.*

A while later, as he stood before the basin with cold water drawn from the wall spigot, he washed his wine glass and said a grace to the kindly wonder who had so mysteriously provided for him. Hanging his work clothes on the wall hooks, he lay down in his underclothes on his narrow bed, shut off the one lamp and, exhausted, went fast to sleep in the dark room.

He regained consciousness of himself, late that afternoon after a long sleep, sitting at the table eating pasta off his plate and drinking a good strong cup of espresso. He didn't know any more how this meal got to his plate than he did others. *Some kind soul is keeping me going. Whoever, I offer my thanks. The boss? A villager? Who knows?*

The dream?

Finished, he leaned back in the chair and recalled some dream fragments in which he, Rizzoli had interrogated himself with questions that then when recalled caused new bewilderment about aspects of his current life and work.

Why don't you know your mama's name or face or, your papa's?

The Uncle, the" important man" who got you hired, why doesn't he visit?

Why do you recall nothing of your first and only walk through the Eternal City?

The Head said you went two years to university but do you know what you studied?

What is the reason for this? Reason? Rizzoli was befuddled and could only laugh, and tell himself: *Here inside the museum, it seems personal details are of no mind compared to gathering each and every one of the tangled aspects of current public and secret history.*

Rizzoli felt freer believing this. He stood, wiped off his plate and cup, scraped crumbs off his table, tossed them in his mouth. He washed up, put on his clothes and stood ready to go to work again.

PART TWO

(1)

In the café on a night in May 1938, Rizzoli saw full-bodied, blond Lena sitting with, Sophia, her aristocratic friend at a table talking, laughing and drinking. They had not been in for awhile. Lena had not yet seen him. Rizzoli watched Lena and recalled the wild, erotic dreams he had ever since meeting her. That first night he had dreamt that they had made love on the bed in the small back room.

When she came to the café, Lena, like the others, did not remember anyone here from before. Rizzoli always remembered to re-introduce himself. Now, he imagined that she desired him anew, as a handsome, young stranger new to her eyes. And he recalled vividly his dreams of lovemaking.

On two prior occasions, when she had urged him to take her off to make love, he had felt the circumstances had not been right. *Tonight!* He told himself.

(2)

Just then a man he knew as a fascist secret police officer shouted. "I can't keep this to myself anymore—I must tell someone. An unknown anarchist intends to assassinate both Hitler and Mussolini when in a few days the German leader will be in Rome for the first time to confer with Mussolini. We in the secret intelligence agency know this. Both will ride in an open car from the airport to central Rome, a 17 mile long ride on a supposedly secret route allowing numerous points for a good marksman to kill both easily."

Easily? Did he say?

"Who, where, when, why, how? We in secret intelligence have no clue as of now. I went to Il Duce and told him we knew of a specific, real threat. He told me that he would be humiliated if he had to tell the Fuhrer that one anarchist had intimidated him into having to change their route. He said, 'I do not believe you.'"

"We Romans all know the route anyway," someone hollered out, "it' s along the streets where new modern fronts are being put on crumbling, ancient houses to make Hitler think the Fascists have brought great progress to this ancient city."

All burst into rousing laughter, including the secret police officer.

The rest of the night Rizzoli was caught up with the others in talk of the planned double assassination. Then he had to go work. Poor Lena.

(3)

After three nights of avoiding the Room of the Head, Rizzoli went in purposely to tell Briganti, "A few days ago, I was blocked from freely exiting the front door. Why?"

Briganti answered with a calm resolve, " You are too important to lose. Think of the vital historical consequences. Once out the door, you'd forget all you've heard in the café as a museum dweller often going there. Even more than my village sources whom you've seen in the café many times but don't recognize, in the future, you will become my best intelligence operative. You go outside and, in a practical sense, you'd forget how to be a janitor. They picked you to change history, the only one."

"That's all well and fine in your mind," answered Rizzoli, " but, the way it works for me is I remember exactly the impersonal aspects of any café-goers talk, but not anything personal like my mama's face or name."

"That's life, Rizzoli."

"Life of the mind, do you mean? Or, in the museum?"

"Both maybe? Maybe both are one. Who can know?"

(4)

Later that night, Rizzoli, with a more comfortable sense of his place in matters, went back to the Room of the Head to talk of another subject. "My feeling is these dictators will start a Second World War. If both die the war will not happen."

"So, if someone kills both these heads of state," Briganti answered, "their nations' wills to expand and dominate the world will collapse, you think?"

"I do. And, frankly, with world tensions lessened, I'd be more likely to die with my prime aim in life fulfilled — of not having…"

"… not having killed a person." Briganti interrupted. "I used to think killing a head of state would change matters, but, not since 1910. Lose the Head, the State will go on, blindly. Generals will lead the innocent humans transformed into wild beasts to war, no matter."

"That's a pessimistic view, Briganti."

"Realistic view, Rizzoli. Yet, not without hope." A pause." Better mankind experience a last, great bloodletting of 50 or 75 million killed. Then the world may be open to the different ways of the village so all can live in cooperation and peace."

"No, Briganti , these two tyrants dead and it saves the peace and all those millions of lives."

"So, Rizzoli, you will not kill yet, you are in favor of an unknown assassin killing two. Doesn't that make you an accomplice of murderous mankind?"

"No. I can't stop the assassin's plans. If I could I would. Have your other sources told anything more?"

"No. My other sources are in the dark, too."

(5)

During the following week, Rizzoli went to the café as much as possible. Lena was not in the café. *Lena, my Lena, where are you?* The room itself, meanwhile, was always full of overlapping voices discussing the possibilities of the dual assassinations, the still unknown, ever more mysterious potential assassin and possible other planners,

Since little was known, Rizzoli heard the cafe crowd voicing only fears, anxieties, or speculations. At times he got confused as to what was fact and fiction, truth and speculation.

Still, he listened intently when, the officer of the fascist secret police said, "You here who have listened to me unburdening myself of the intense but hidden worry of my dilemma in not solving this pending assassination plot, I wish to thank you, Even though once out of this café, none of you will remember. Nor will I."

Nor will I, did he say? Rizzoli asked himself.

"Here are the facts," the officer went on. "First, the route from the airport is so long that it affords a good marksman, with a long distance sight and accurate rifle, every chance of killing them both. Over that parade distance the likely near and far hidden vantage points for the shooter are nearly incalculable. What we know signals to me he is an expert shot. Mussolini continues to deny all of this and calls me a fool for telling him."

Shouts rang out. "Il Duce's the Fool!" "Bald Benito the Bold!" "All Hail, Our Joker-Tyrant!" "May the bullet be true to those two!"

The officer smiled. Rizzoli sensed this response was not what the officer needed.

"Find this anarchist son of a bitch, that's your job, isn't it?" shouted another man. *I had always guessed that man was an antifascist. Goes to show it's hard to tell who's who in the café.* "Do your job!"

The officer dropped his head at that remark. Rizzoli felt a slight pity for him.

The next afternoon, in the café, the rumor was that the officer had committed suicide. None could substantiate it. Rizzoli felt it must be true.

(6)

The night before the day of the Fuhrer's arrival to join Il Duce in the open car parade, the café was electric with anticipation. Would the two tyrants live or die? Lena was there. *Lena!* Countess Sophia sat next to her.

Going over to Lena, he re-introduced himself and could tell by the look in her eyes that she lusted for him.

"I'm Lena, " she said in a cool voice. "I don't know you but I'm glad to meet. Please sit down and pour some wine. This is the Countess Sophia." *I am experiencing an exact, prior moment, yes?*

In time, she began rubbing Rizzoli's thigh. This time he led her to the bed in the café's back room where the two made love the rest of the night. Time after time, they consummated their lovemaking—on top of the red and black checkered bedspread, on the over stuffed chair, on the white and black tiled floor, against the blue wall, door, and back wall, and on the wooden chair with him sitting her straddling. Again just before dawn, once more on the bed with both exhausted. Then she had to leave.

Rizzoli went out the back door, down the hall into his room, fell on his bed and slept a long while. He awoke and thought, *I've slept the sleep of the dead. But, wait! I've missed my shift for the first time.* He was aghast. Then he remembered Lena. Oh, Lena! All that pent-up desire and finally they make love. Next time, he would have to start over, reintroduce myself once again as a stranger magnetizing her and—what then?

(7)

The dual assassination! He remembered the historic visit was today. Immediately, hurriedly, he went to the café, not knowing what to expect. A newspaper on the table had a headline: "Great Leaders Saved: Brothel Madam Sleeps In!" The photo was of Lena. *Lena?*

Rizzoli read that Lena was supposed to wake up her youngest girl, who was to have awakened the anarchist, Giancarlo, who was bent on killing both Mussolini and Hitler. But, the madam had slept in, after a late, wild night of her own. Out of frustration at missing his date with destiny, Giancarlo went into a rage, wrecking the brothel out of frustration. When police arrived, he killed three with a handgun before he was killed in a scene of chaotic anarchy.

A side story had a sub-headline:" Love and Anarchy: Foil the Plot." It told of Giancarlo and the young prostitute falling madly in love and making love all night on the certainty that he would die in the morning after killing the two world leaders.

Rizzoli knew that because he made love to Lena all night, he had prevented the dual assassination. In view of that failure, he, Rizzoli, felt solely responsible for personally being the root cause of any coming of the Second World War that he had predicted and Briganti had stated would kill millions and millions and mutilate millions more.

He felt an immediate and terrible personal guilt for the consequences for mankind of his own personal lust. *How could I do this?* Rizzoli felt terrible *It was my own lust. That's no excuse. None. It is me, and me alone. I cannot forget the effect of my actions on history. Until my death, I will be history's captive.*

That night he told Briganti everything: that his and Lena's mutual lust led to the all-night love-making that caused Lena not to wake her girl to wake the anarchist who was to kill both vile dictators, an act almost certain to have prevented any possible coming war.

"Briganti, hear me. I, Rizzoli, no one else, must accept responsibility for any future war caused by these two monstrous dictators. I, Rizzoli, who wanted to die without killing a single person, will be the prime cause of a horrendous bloodletting war."

"If you want to think in this narrow way," answered Briganti, " you, Rizzoli, have already indirectly killed four — the anarchist and three policeman. Why? You would have to say, yours and Lena's lust. But, I know you can think about this another way..."

Already four persons are dead! Briganti is right, I wasn't thinking about the immediate consequences — I'm responsible for multiple killings, then a world war. Rizzoli felt terrible. " It's like I've got some curse, Briganti..."

"Rizzoli, hear me, none of us can predict and most humans can't know or, won't acknowledge the true consequences – long term — of their actions.

"But Briganti, I know my actions and accept the complete responsibility for the results."

"Rizzoli, as the common man, you think in this straight-on fashion. As the intellectual, I think in a zigzag manner. I can help you here. Listen, war has high odds of occurring anytime, anywhere, always. I'll grant you, Hitler and Il Duce surviving keep it at decent odds."

"There, Briganti, you have come around? No?"

"No. Nothing you or any single person could do will change that. A will to war is always a possibility, given mankind has not evolved far enough to refuse it. If a future war does erupt, it will be the result of consequences so complex, it could never be traced back to just one cause, believe me."

"I can't see that. You lost me."

"Naturally, Rizzoli, as the common man, you must dismiss my view as up-in-the-clouds and see the truth as being clear and down to earth, like you said — if war comes, your lust makes you personally responsible. Right?"

NO ZIGZAG LOGIC FOR ME? "It's you who seems to know the whole plot in this."

"Well, myself, I say, good for yours and Lena's mutual lust."

"*Why?*" Rizzoli was flabbergasted. *Why?*

"I'll give in to your thinking," Briganti said. "You are likely to cause war, right?"

"You've got it "

"A horrendous war."

"Yes."

"Yet, this is fine. One, it will finally make all surviving humans beg for a lasting peace. Two, thus, after the war the Village will re-seed humanity." Briganti paused. "This makes you a great anti-hero of history — the catalyst who will bring the disaster necessary for the creating of the greater good for all mankind."

Who's what? Anti-hero?

"Me? Did you call me some sort of hero? No, I'd say, more of a villain." (*I'm reasoning out loud like Briganti. Dammit!*) "Wouldn't you say?" Before the Head can answer, he continued. " Not a willing villain, for sure, Briganti, but, you see, more of one, than any hero—that is to my common man's way of thinking."

"So, if you see yourself as a villain—be a villain, make up excuses for yourself, blame this Lena for the lust," Briganti answered, "You convince yourself, she treated you as her mere pawn and lured you into lust and war."

" No. Never. She bears no personal responsibility. Her lust, thus, was pure. Me? I did remember her from before and thus, have the burden of acting on all the lust..."

"Lust is not a burden. Enjoy it, Rizzoli. I can only lust in my mind, as I'm an intellectual, severed Head, You are the full-bodied common man so lust, lust all you can. Forget consequences."

Rizzoli was stunned. "At the cost of a world war?"

"Yes! If your reasoning proves true, I repeat my response, the world's slaughter you cause is only the price for the greater good."

Rizzoli yearned for redemption—*my one hope is Briganti's certainty—after the war his visionary prehistoric village re-seeds the world with a more evolved strain of humanity. May Briganti be right, so help me.*"

Briganti changed the subject abruptly. "Your Lena, now. I hope the Fascists won't kill her."

" No, she didn't know her girl had been hiding him. Besides, the Black Shirts are fond of Lena, her brothel and especially her girls. Lena hates the Fascists. She will get them drunk and get secrets from them."

"Good. All is well that ends well."

Ends well, I need to believe Briganti. Rizzoli felt this sudden, deep fondness towards his friend, the old Head. *He's becoming my only recourse for a good father.*

PART THREE

(1)

Rizzoli lay on his bed musing on a mid-September afternoon in 1943 when those words uttered by the Head in 1938 came to mind. *Ends well.* In 1939, Hitler had started this World War. In recent days Briganti had said that "on all fronts, the end of the war and the start of peace are approaching. Much fighting remains, but that all will go on to a final peace." Rizzoli felt reassured. *All that goes well. Ends well. My redemption is the nature of the final peace.* Rizzoli had come to believe this unquestionably over the years of slaughter.

Starting with their forces landing in Sicily on July 10, 1943, the Allies had opened a new front. The village outliers had been the first to report to Briganti that the Allies would soon invade the mainland and move up the Italian peninsula, aiming to liberate Naples, then Rome.

Under this initial allied threat, the King reacted in an astonishing way. This news was not yet public when Rizzoli witnessed a turncoat high official and "friend" to Il Duce enter the café and loudly and jovially voice the state secret that, with the majority vote of the Fascist Grand Council, the King had dismissed and imprisoned Mussolini and appointed a new prime minister, Marshall Brodoglio!

Rizzoli told Briganti the news. The café crowd had erupted in ringing cheers when the official had yelled, "The dictatorship is over! His Fascism is no more!"

Briganti laughed uproariously. "The blind crowd doesn't see it. The King wants only to try to save the monarchy. And Brodoglio! He was the Fascist general who made his reputation secretly using batches of illegal gas."

Soon the new prime minister, Briganti learned, had signed a secret truce and then surrendered to the Allies in Naples. Defeat, then betrayal. With that the Italian State in Rome vanished. Its high officials fled to Allied safety. No King. No prime minister. No generals to give orders to the soldiers.

"The State is Headless," Briganti said, laughing. "Long live the State." Rizzoli laughed, too. In the following weeks, a series of dire consequences unfolded, each conveyed in Briganti's visions.

Countless German soldiers invaded Italy, killing those of a now turncoat enemy. Soon Nazis occupied Rome and the peninsula farther south to fight the Allied advance north to Rome. Ordinary Italian soldiers, abandoned without orders, fled, everyone to their own destinies. The Nazi occupied part of the country became dangerous—every man for himself, trust no one became the motto. The Germans targeted many among the millions left behind, sudden refugees in their own country.

The Head routinely responded in a characteristic manner. "Let's not get distracted. Focus on the Allied armies, being stalled at times, yes, but breaking through to continue their drive north to liberate Rome and free us from this terrible occupation by the Nazis."

Il Duce, rescued from prison by the Nazis, had started a rump Fascist state in the far north of Italy, by Lake Garda, called The Republic of Salo, propped up by the Germans. Italian fighters either went north to fight with his reconstituted Fascist Army; south to fight with the Allies or, finally, north and everywhere to fight as the anti-fascist guerrilla resistance.

(2)

One evening in October 1943, Rizzoli was in his room immersed in complete darkness. His one light had dimmed, then gone out. *It's either another bombing blackout or electrical failure. No matter.* He had his ways to make do.

Bastard Germans occupying Rome, their brutality terrifies ordinary persons. The occupiers control the electricity. Daily, they roundup Romans, they accuse of resistance, murder them far outside the old city walls and bury them in mass graves. We civilians trapped here, they want to slowly starve us. Bent to the blind will of these occupiers, I feel even more my fate as a captive of history.

His room had no windows for light, so, in the pitch black, he felt his way and took his cup from a hook on the wall. He opened the small tin of ersatz espresso, sprinkled a bit in the cup and added cold water from the spout. With a spoon, he stirred and tasted this cold, flat, bitter, chicory-flavored brew. Awful, but never would he complain, *as all Romans are grateful for anything, even cheap substitutes, now that the Italian war effort has failed and food supplies are low.*

Moving away from the sink, he went a few steps to the table to see if the still mysterious source had left even a few bits of food. Sometimes, now, there was nothing given the wartime shortages of almost everything. His finger found a few morsels on the plate—bits of stale, hard cheese and dried bread. He ate these and was pleased to have something in his stomach before he laid down for his nap before going to work.

On his bed, with his single cover pulled over him, he heard planes overhead, *Likely German bombers, from their engine sounds, flying south to hit Allied troops on their way north soon to liberate Rome.*

The Head had steadily emphasized to Rizzoli that after the war, a new world for mankind would arise. This helped Rizzoli to lighten his burden of blame for being one of the causes of this war. *Only the Head and I know that my lustful night with Lena had helped cause the war. Now the dictators are fighting on the defensive and the Head believes their ultimate defeat will bring lasting peace and the redemption of mankind. And, my own absolution, I hope.*

First, the liberation of Rome, Rizzoli thought, lying there. The Americans will be here soon. Yes! The Fedora Fascist is furious at the Allied advance and the retreat of his great Il Duce. And the Soviet armies are driving back the Nazi forces in the East to the dismay of the Fuhrer.

(3)

Awakening still in the darkness, he slowly went about his routines: putting on his same work clothes, going to the hallway closet for his broom and dust pan then, still by touch and memory, up the flight of stairs to the museum. Thoughtfully, looking into the room's pure blackness, he pictured the places of each of his favorite display cases and the criminals in it.

All these criminals he referred to in his own familiar and rather fond way—Beppo the Brigand, Enzo the Magnificent Swindler. His favorite was Vincenzo Perrugia, who had stolen the *Mona Lisa* from the Louvre on August 22, 1911 and kept it until 1914. *Vincenzo the Great! Yes.* As he neatly swept around their displays, he had his usual thought: *All these are innocents compared to this day's prime wartime aggressors and mass killers: Hitler and Mussolini.*

Briganti the Light! Why hadn't I thought of him before now? Whenever the electricity went off, he usually thought automatically of the wiring keeping his old beheaded friend alive. He took his broom and ran to burst into Briganti's room.

Having switched him to the small, temporary generator recently, Rizzoli checked to see if he had done all the wiring hook-ups right. One by one he reassured himself. *Yes.* He dispelled the sudden fear that, by his mistake, he could harm the Head. Confident now, he called into Briganti.

"Rizzoli, so good to hear your voice. What have you heard in the cafe? Rome will be liberated soon, right?"

" All expect the Americans will be in Rome soon. But, I hear nothing definite. The café, there I hear Italians state that out in reality, many countrymen have become a betraying treacherous lot for the sake of survival. Once big time fascists tell of plans to hide their former identities, go to the hills and join the armed resistance in the North. What do you hear from your sources, Briganti?"

"I hear much the same, Rizzoli. Soldiers who remained die-hard fascists joined the fugitive Mussolini in his tiny fascist state propped up by the Germans. The Resistance also has grown with added former official soldiers. Civilians caught in the middle of course are suffering the most, as first one side then the other accuse the old, women and babies of harboring the enemy. Killing innocents or burning villages is the result. Hurry Allies. Hurry."

"Yes, Briganti, what's the Village like in these times?"

"The Village has appeared like a Talkie Movie Village inside my Head for years. Villagers, now long-time friends there, have appeared and spoken with me almost daily for years close up amidst the hustle bustle of the secret place. All are in the know about the ancient magic formula for transforming any intruder into something productive or beautiful."

"The village 'guardians' mostly have been in the 'real' outside world, now like Tommaso's cell and another outlier cell, and are constantly on the alert for the world discovering and endangering the village. Recently he, as the leader of both outlier cells, has come here to report to me events from the outside the museum, from Rome, of course, then, Italy and Europe."

"Sure, your tie with the Village dates from way back," Rizzoli interrupted, "when you had the visitation and became the new Briganti The Light?"

" True. True. Now in these treacherous times, they have Tommaso and a few others of his young group outside in

Rome in modern guise looking to gain top-secret information to help protect their beloved village. This outlier cell will also hope soon after the war to be the seeds to change the global world into the peaceful ways of the village. So man will be the redemption of mankind." The Head paused. Rizzoli felt deeply moved.

One late night a month or so later, Rizzoli plugged into Briganti and heard only forlorn sobbing sounds echoing inside his skull. "What is it? Briganti! What? It's Rizzoli, tell me."

After some time, with Rizzoli anxious, Briganti's weeping died down. As Rizzoli looked at the Head draped in sagging yellow skin, the words in its mind came slowly, haltingly to tell Rizzoli that "Nazi bombers had destroyed the whole village and that a Nazi patrol had ambushed and killed the whole village reconnaissance cell, including Tommaso."

AM I, Rizzoli, as the sole constant museum living friend of the Head, the only one left who can converse with his mind voice, offering him just my own tid-bits of cafe knowledge? Me? Only? Rizzoli felt an aching sympathy. *Briganti!*

(4)

During his shift, one night in late winter 1944, Rizzoli tuned in to Briganti and instantly sensed the sad mood of the old head. "Aside from the elimination of Tommaso's first cell," Briganti stated right off, "the second smaller village cell did survive. And these new sources are of the view that the Allies plan to permanently dig in at the river to the south where they've halted for the winter."

Rizzoli did not interrupt, but now he rejoiced, "Briganti, the second cell did survive! Isn't that good news amidst this long Nazi-Allied fight for the Italian peninsula?"

"Yes but this remaining cell has intelligence that the German resistance is so fierce that the Allies plan to tie down the Germans and think a spring offensive too costly to liberate Rome. What do you hear, Rizzoli?"

"Briganti, I've never heard or read anything to that effect."

"Maybe so. But, don't you think Rome could be devastated if its liberation is put off for all that time until Germany surrenders." He paused. " The surviving cell does lift my spirits. These youthful ones do remain positive that no matter the timing or the situation, the total Allied victory will be at the exact right time for the new birth of humanity." His voice broke as he added, " Too many millions have died for humanity not to see this war as a turning point in world history, you agree?

" I do. I do." said Rizzoli. .

"Listen, keep your head up, my old friend", Rizzoli continued. "Matters are not that bad. Yes, the liberation is taking longer than we Romans all hoped. In the café, some make jokes about what will take the longer, The Second Coming or the Allied Liberation. Odds are on the latter, 5 to 1. But, it is coming any day. Don't lose hope"

"Rizzoli, life long — with or without a body — the hope of this better earthly world to come has sustained me. I can't hold on much longer."

"You hold on. Hear me! All these Allies air raids on the far outskirts and in outlying farm-lands of Rome hardly mean the liberators plan to stay in place. No, the planes are knocking out German positions, for the American ground forces to come into Rome."

"Who knows, Rizzoli? But, as a quick change of subject, do you remember Lena?"

"Are you still lusting for each other, writhing about on the old bed?

" Yes, of course, and afterwards she always asks, "Now tell me your name so I can remember?"

Briganti laughed. "What a joy! You two writhing and loving even with Nazi bombers going over and explosions sounding.

"What else? I can't help myself."

"That's the way. Keep on. You two give me hope in, the good ordinary man and woman, loving and enduring all this."

(5)

The lights suddenly went off. Darkness. Then, Rizzoli heard the distant bombs exploding, killing, injuring, maiming, tormenting — almost indiscriminately — Allied soldiers and almost certainly innocent common men and women, young, old, infants, dogs, cats, horses, cows, goats. *Briganti can't hear the war or see the dark. No need to tell him.*

Generator is off! Rizzoli tried frantically to get it going again. "There. It's on! " He then found the necessary life supports for The Head in good order. After a long time of calling to him, he had no success. *Briganti dead?*

"Briganti? BRIGANTI?" [His voice echoed faintly then faded out.]

"No answer! No answer! No, no!" Rizzoli started sobbing and feeling light-headed and missing his one friend. "No one but me left living in the museum?"

He still listened for any signs of life lingering inside the dying Head. Rizzoli did hear Briganti's murmuring mind voice come back once. But, only to utter a salad mix of nonsense words, phrases and once even murmur a jumbled sentence. Then, no more, only silence—he was brain dead. Rizzoli sobbed.

After Rizzoli had gathered himself together, he concluded that Briganti in his last days had felt most distressed at forgetting large sequences of his previously remembered grand overview of the last years of history, leading up to and including the war. Thus, the whole of that vast story was making less and less sense to him.

This would be as Rizzoli had always suspected— *Briganti's Mind was for storing the whole of the span of that history and he, Rizzoli, and the various Village sources were mere couriers of that history, each one a different, particular and partial cord of Briganti's vast history.*

I even came to the conclusion Briganti could accurately predict say five or ten years into the future from these past trends. " Now he's dead."

Suddenly, Rizzoli heard the muted pops of guns fired somewhere. He rubbed his eyes, gazed at the Head. Transfixed for the moment, he himself had a feeling of lightness coming over him. Why? He didn't know, but he felt as if some parts of his own particular memory of the years of conflict and war had vanished, freeing him of bearing some of the weight of that history.

(6)

A while later, back in his room, Rizzoli looked up and saw a person whom he maybe recognized. *He must have come in while I had my head down thinking about Briganti. Tommaso, is it? Alive? Is he?*

"Tommaso?" *Can't be.* "You and all your resistance cell died in an ambush."

"We did. I was dead. People believe I'm dead. I came back to life with others to help with the post-war rebirth of true mankind. Here, feel the bullet hole in my side."

His voice doesn't sound familiar, Rizzoli cautioned himself. *I only talked to him that once. I'll put my finger in the bullet hole in his heart.* He did. It was deep; his finger felt the other's heart beating. *It's proof. It's him.*

"Listen, first I need to tell you," said Tommaso, "I just came from Briganti's room and he's back alive, conversing. You saved his life, thanks to your work with the generator." "Fantastic! Yes!" hollered Rizzoli. "And for that," he continued, "The Head said that he owed you. What? I don't know."

'Anyway I and the other stranded villagers are preparing important work to do after the war" Tommaso continued. "I know you will keep that in strict confidence between the two of us."

" I will and do appreciate the visit" Rizzoli answered. "I hope all of you and Briganti's expectations are proven right so that at war's end, a new peaceful global era will start. And this idealism proves possible, you know, Tommaso?"

"I do. Whenever I've a doubt, and I do, I ask my mind, 'Were you ever really dead, Tommaso?' I know the answer. You felt the hole in my heart, Rizzoli. That erases all my doubt."

Ask his mind? Did he say?

"Oh, before I forget, I need to tell you, Rizzoli, that for the time being, Briganti is still a little muddled in the head, after his nearing death experience. And Oh, Oh, the other thing is…. The form of his being has shifted " *Form? Shifted?* Tommaso continued, "Nothing really to be concerned about. And remember, his mind is still a bit addled, naturally, coming out of that experience, huh?"

(7)

After Tommaso left, Rizzoli was excited and went straight up to see and talk with his old friend Briganti. "Hello!" He hollered into the receiver. "Hello, Briganti! What a pleasure to have you back. It's me, Rizzoli?"

" Frizzoli? Did you say?"

"Rizzoli"

"Rizzoli, that's what I said?"

Said Frizzoli.

In that brief exchange, Rizzoli realized that Briganti's new "form of being" involved his mind voice being outside his skull, and bouncing around from place to place in the room, seeming to speak from the ceiling, then wall, then floor. The tone was matter-of-fact. Rizzoli could just listen to the Head's mind voice zigzag around the room talking. He set the receiver down and listened.

"Listen, in my near death experience, I was outside my skull looking down on it from within a bright lighted aura and a enlightening vision came to me about our past relationship. Here it is: you are "alive" only in my imagination. I was telling a story to entertain myself and imagined you a prime character. You were, and are now, a little Rizzoli seen in my mind's eye."

"A little Rizzoli, did you say?" *Briganti's gone cuckoo, sure as hell and why not, he's gone out of his skull, lost in his Mind.*

"Yes, but, Rizzoli is only a name I picked out of the blue."

"Liguria was your home, only because I stated that, but to you, it is only a name, located you can't know where, as you are 'alive' only inside my mind." (*Lunatic's mind is wobbling all over the goddamn place!*)

"You had a mother and father but I gave them no names or physical descriptions, so, to you, in the story, both are nameless and featureless." *I'll tell you who is featureless, a loopy mind out of its head bouncing off walls. His brain is addled, all right.*

"You are a figment of the living memory of me, Rizzoli. In my inner mind I made you up with words." (*Must think he's Napoleon now, before Elba*) "...an exact number needed to describe your character—appearance, dialogue, thoughts, actions—for my own entertainment and to kill time. In my now waning memory, I recall and then forget you. Before I forget you completely and your 'life' withers away..."

(*Speak for yourself, Mr. Who-Who.*)

"... without a trace, I owe you because you saved my life. You will live a life even if your character's 'life' dies in my inner mind."

"I have a life now and am living it now, and will continue to live it, no matter what you've said about me."

"So you say you are a free self?" was the only response Rizzoli could muster out of the disembodied mind. Rizzoli took a breath. "The museum here has been my life since 1938 — for the past six years. Sure it's been a chaotic, contradictory, paradoxical existence. But within these walls, I felt I had a role in a larger scheme of life. Your certainty of the coming post-war world of peace dissolved my chaos, eased my guilt at being a captive of this war's tragic, history. You made this my home, at any rate. You were...are still my best friend."

"And you are still my best friend," the now set-in-place, no longer bouncing mind uttered, in a shaky, weepy voice. "It was your home. But, we can't ever go back to the way it was. The only constant in life is change and life owes us that, huh?"

"Uh-huh."

Briganti had reverted to a normal, rational, very sane way of talking. "Remember this, Rizzoli, the post-war world will become the one of global peace and, in it, you will fare well."

Rizzoli had no answer. He was as confused at the beginning as at the end of Briganti's crazed ramble and then suddenly sensible talk.

(8)

In this late spring of 1944, the café was empty and completely in the dark. Rizzoli was alone. But he sensed someone else was here, too. He even thought he could see someone's shadowy outline.

When I walked in, the café wasn't in the dark, was it? He couldn't remember the lights going out, *only that I had been in the dark since finding myself in here. Finding myself? Whenever that was. Whatever it means.*

Suddenly, Rizzoli heard a shadowy someone talking to himself in a low voice expressing something far across the room. *It's the Fedora Fascist. You know the sound of his voice.*

Wait! That's Briganti's voice talking inside my mind, isn't it? Briganti answered, *Yes my voice is in your head temporarily because I had to warn you in private and not be overheard by you-know-who is also in this café.* Rizzoli was astounded that Briganti was out of his room for the first time ever. *At least his voice.*

Careful, friend, the Fedora Fascist is armed and dangerous, he has a real pistol loaded and wants to kill. Be careful. I'm not sure I can help you given my own fast changing context. With me suddenly gone out of my head; then into your Head that means all is changing. I'm convinced, things are now in the midst of changing to be more real — the Fascist can shoot and kill.

Briganti told Rizzoli what the fascist was thinking to himself this instant; and the two listened to the third man's mind say " *I do know beyond any doubt there is in here right now a person — I don't know exactly whom — but this vile bastard lives in the museum, often frequents the café and in all his many times past in the café has never forgotten what was revealed or by whom at any time.*

Briganti interjects to say, *I used to know almost all those revelations, but since my nearly dying I've forgotten many of all the café goers secrets. But I do remember the circumstance that made you the post-war redeemer of mankind and why the village selected you.* Rizzoli added. *Many of my café reports to you I've forgotten as well.*

The Fedora Fascist vowed, " At the point of a gun, I'll drive this would be betrayer outside for the first time in years so he forgets all secrets. If he should dare refuse, I'll kill him."

Rizzoli now realized his own mind was without Briganti's voice. It had fled. Rizzoli was scared. *The gun is real, but am I? Or am I still fiction?* In his preoccupation, Rizzoli had lost track of where the shadowy third man had gone. All seemed empty in the café. Silent.

He looked around. He couldn't locate him. Rizzoli took three steps further into the café. Something stirred.

Having hidden behind the museum bar, the Fedora Fascist was now standing, leaning forward on the bar top pointing a pistol at Rizzoli and saying, "State your secret, Rizzoli. You have never done so!"

"My actions made this war possible."

"Bastard, you made war possible and, thus, Il Duce is now near defeat because you began the war." He paused. "Without war he would still rule in Rome and all of Italy and over a great empire. He and the Fuhrer would be the world's leaders." He grimly held up the pistol, aiming to kill Rizzoli.

Then the Fedora Fascist vanished and a potted corn stalk stood there on the bar top where the gunman was leaning forward about to shoot only seconds ago. His pistol leaned against it.

Rizzoli turned and saw Tommaso at a café table, smiling up at the corn stalk and pistol reflected in reverse image in the back mirror of the bar and there Tommaso's face also appeared in the same reverse way. Then Tommaso turned, smiling and wandered out the front door and vanished into the streets of ... 1944 Rome?

Rizzoli was happy. Coming to his mind again was Briganti's voice saying, *Tommaso demonstrated right then the old village way of magically transforming a potential tyrant into a harmless form of nature or of beauty.*

Rizzoli went to the front of the bar top and in the back mirror viewed his own image reflected with the pistol leaning against the corn stalk — the bodily remains of the transformed Fedora Fascist.

Hard to tell what is real.

(9)

"Liberation Day Today. The Germans Out of Rome." This was the main headline on a newspaper in the brightly lit café. Another read: "Fighting to the North. Allies to Enter Rome."

Outside, he could hear all Romans, it seemed, gathered in vast crowds repeatedly cheering, singing, giving loud toasts and laughing raucously. Colorful balloons hung in the air with confetti. A few handed out pamphlets for the new political parties. *Everyone has to be out celebrating.*

Everyone, that is, but, me. I'll sit down, drink, listen and have my own celebration until it gets dark. He sat, drank his wine and got drunk.

Earlier, when he had entered the café, it was lit but empty of people or waiters, bartender. Everyone. Deserted. All were outside celebrating. He felt very lonely. *Briganti seemed to have disappeared altogether.* But at the same moment on the bar top, he noticed someone had left a ready bottle of wine with the cork out and a waiting glass, next to the potted corn. The pistol was gone. He filled the glass up with a deep red. He finished that and had another. Silently, he toasted the crowd outside.

In a while, Briganti's strange voice filled the room: "I have lost my grasp of history, it is true, but possibly now that has made me a seer who goes into a trance spell and hears and sees matters that tell of the future. I've had a few such strange experiences."

"I don't suppose you're going to reveal any," Rizzoli said.

"The Resistance will soon capture Il Duce dressed as a woman with his mistress Clara trying to run away. Partisans will execute them and hang both corpses upside down in public view at a petrol station."

Rizzoli found this preposterous. *Briganti has lost his mind again. Poor bastard.*

The voice paused and went on.

"The Fuhrer and his mistress Eva will both take poison and commit suicide in his Berlin Bunker."

Hearing these wild predictions, Rizzoli strangely felt less ensnared in the making of the terrible history of his time. Humiliating deaths for these two dictators — his original 1938 antagonists — would bring his mind relief from its complicity in not letting the assassin do his task. Millions are dead because of those two monstrous dictators. At that, he choked up with tears. *Millions.*

Rizzoli broke down and wept until he was gasping.

After a while, he calmed as beloved memories came forth of Briganti's Head, whose once great mind was the grand repository of current history and of how forgiving the Head had been in promising him, Rizzoli, some type of redemption as an anti-hero who uses tragedy to teach humanity its foremost lesson of life, to live.

Briganti's spirit voice moving into different places made Rizzoli think of the leftover empty skull. *What will happen to the Head's mere skull even if its spirit goes?* He didn't dare ask, *What is its fate? Undiscovered and left behind? Or gone? Stored? Destroyed?* He balked at asking Briganti.

(10)

Impulsively, he got up, walked toward the front door, grasped the handle, paused a long moment and recalled the instance before when a force kept him from crossing this threshold, stopped him going one step further. *Would the outside keep me inside again?* Closing his eyes, he pushed down on the door handle and held the door open while he struggled to take that one, difficult step over the threshold. He did.

Opening his eyes, he gazed into the spring brightness and felt the sun's warmth on his skin. Am I real? He bit his lip. It bled. Yes.

Instantly, Briganti's voice was talking inside Rizzoli's mind.

"You becoming real makes me ecstatic, too, Rizzoli. Listen, here is my problem—my voice needs a vessel, a host body's mind, Otherwise my spirit voice will fade and evaporate into nothing. Will you do me the favor I've done you and let me live?"

"Let's be clear, you're not saying my own mind voice will be replaced by your mind, are you, Briganti?" Rizzoli asked.

"No, never, you would be of two minds, so to speak. See, I am in this position because the villagers found it impossible to bring me back to earth from death to be one of them because my body had been separated from my head for so long, so many years. It was lost dust. So, I needed to find a vessel to be in.

"I could host your mind," said Rizzoli, "but, first, can you give me some specific details—say, omens that spell out the coming World's "new order" of peace and cooperation for a decade after the end of war? Granted now Rome has been liberated, but much fighting remains in the world before that peace."

"I'll try. As a trance-seer now, I go under a spell and say words, phrases, a sentence or two or describe an image or a vision that predestines the conditions of the postwar world."

"I'm listening," said Rizzoli.

"'Free World' will be a term of reference used daily around the globe by all living on earth. 'United Nations' is another; it will be an organization that keeps world peace. An image came to me of its vast headquarters building by a wide river. 'The Universal Declaration of the Rights of Man' will be passed by a united world to guarantee the protection of the human rights and dignity of every individual on earth."

"History will end; no longer a nightmare. Oh, and Tommaso and the remaining villagers will transform likely future tyrants into things of benefit to mankind."

" Mankind finally relieved of war by the horror of this war."

Someone in the crowd offered Rizzoli a pamphlet; instinctively he took it.

He glanced back. The large front doors were padlocked. A sign read: "MUSEUM CLOSED since 8 May 1940." Did that mean that for years, as he worked, the public was locked out and the only ones ever to be on the exhibit floor were Rizzoli, the village spies, and the Head? The café was the only place open to the public.

Aside from this question, Rizzoli felt overwhelmed by the brilliant weather that melted him into one with the joyous crowd. His face warmed to the sun.

Glancing down at the pamphlet, he saw it was translated into Italian from English, but he saw "Anarchist's..." in the banner at the top and assumed it was a handout to support that political party. Briganti started reading. It was nonsense to Rizzoli, but Briganti's mind voice read then kept stopping to exclaim: "I can't believe it. This is incredible." Then he'd read on. Rizzoli had no patience for listening anymore; the context was confusing and his joined mind's voice was annoying, but kept on and on.

In contrast, Rizzoli felt *real*. Ignoring the reading, he waded in and got lost in the crowd. Feeling the breeze on his face was divine. He wanted to lose himself in life.

Briganti's voice went on and on.

Rizzoli rushed to join the celebration in the street. As he waded deeper into the crowd, Rizzoli felt liberated. *Ecstatic. Alive!* Most of all, free, and eager to witness a new mankind after the war.

May 12, 2007

Anarchist's Head Is Finally Buried, but Outcry Arises Over Timing

ROME, May 11 — The anarchist Giovanni Passannante is becoming a cause célèbre 97 years after his death.

Until this week Mr. Passannanante's skull and brain, preserved in formaldehyde, were on display at a criminology museum in Rome in what ranked as one of Italy's more macabre showcases. In this museum-loving society, it was a strange fate for someone who tried to kill the king of Italy 120 years ago.

At Mr. Passannante's death, his head and brain were removed to be studied by sociologists, in keeping with the scientific eugenicist theory made popular at that time by a criminologist named

Cesare Lombroso. He believed that criminality was inherited and could be identified by physical traits.

For the last 70 years the brain and skull have been in a display case, framed by old anarchist manifests on the second floor of the Criminology Museum, just off Via Giulia.

The skull and brain were to leave the museum on Friday, in front of reporters and photographers, for burial with the body after pressure from hundreds of petition signers. But, instead, on Thursday, the remnants were whisked away secretly and buried in his hometown in the Basilicata region of southern Italy.

It was supposed to be the final chapter in a story lasting for decades, pitting leftist intellectuals against Italy's dwindling traditionalist monarchists. Instead, it added further intrigue to the pitiable legacy of Mr. Passannante.

"It's terrible," said Ulderico Pesce, an artist who had led the campaign to bury all of Mr. Passannante. Mr. Pesce was speaking by phone from the cemetery in Savoia Lucania, where the remains were buried Thursday night and where, he said, a crowd of onlookers had formed Friday morning.

Mr. Pesce was baffled and angered by the decision to bury Mr. Passannante a day earlier than had been announced. "He was buried like an empty bottle," he said. He is still seeking a proper, public burial for the skull and brain. In a statement the regional government said the date was changed for security reasons and out of " feelings of human pity."

Mr. Passannante earned a place in Italian history in 1878 by trying to assassinate King Umberto I of Savoy. (Umberto was later assassinated by another anarchist.) Mr. Passannante was arrested tortured and given a death sentence that was later reduced to life *in prison. His family was jailed. His hometown, Salvia, changed its name to Savoia di Lucania.*

As the tale goes, Mr. Passannante was jailed on the island of Elba. He remained in solitary confinement and went insane. In 1910, he was sent to an asylum and died shortly after. In 1998 Oliviero Diliberto, the minister of justice at the time, wrote the decree allowing for the removal of Mr. Passannante's remains to his hometown.

That eight years elapsed before the local authorities responded, prompted speculation that Mr. Passannante's sin was not yet absolved.

"No one wanted to deal with this case," said Vito De Filippo, president of the Basilicata region. Others see nefarious forces at work. Mr. Pesce lays the blame at the foot of Lucania's mayor, Rossina Ricciardii, who he asserts was under pressure to delay the burial.

Repeated calls to the mayor's office were not returned.

Mr. De Filippo said he saw something else in the story.

"Passannante is a symbol of the south," he said, "and while everything is not resolved and the south has many problems, we have the civility to close this story, by bringing him home."[1]

"… we have the civility to close this story, by bringing him home."

The newspaper article ended on that thought. Rizzoli tore the paper into strips, as his other mind hollered, *No, Stop!* He threw the confetti into the air.

No!

---

[1] *The New York Times,* May 12, 2007.

Shut up!

You shut up!

Make me!

You think my mind can't rule over your mind, Briganti? Try me.

The Mirror of Antiquity

(1)

Monday morning.

Rizzoli opens his bedroom door. While moving to its backside with the full-length mirror, he glimpses his image coming into view more on the reflecting surface. A loud street noise distracts him before he focuses squarely on the mirror for one last check before he's out the door. *Who's that?*

In the mirror, he sees an upright freak creature, half animal *who from the waist down is a rear half of a goat in all its glory*, black balls dangling, down with a sheaved dick, *a Billy Goat? With powerful ramrod, rear thighs coated with straight dark hair. What is this?*

And who from his waist up, is a half man — with a muscular belly, chest, arms—all covered with a thin down of dark hair; his upper body looks powerful. His face *big, round, dark bearded, … Can it be the creature from myth, a Satyr? Stands for uninhibited lust. A Satyr! Sure.*

Has to be, poking up out of his thick mat of tangled, dark hair, the man even has little horns and pointed ears. Rizzoli fixes on his eyes, captivated, as *these seem demonic, sideways slits of gold pupils in the round black. Staring, the weird eyes give a leering look, don't they?*

The Satyr's face, otherwise, has an eerily yearning look. Upright. *He's standing on what?* Rizzoli squints at the bottom of the mirror … *two, hard, split hooves; down at the end of thin calves.*

The creature has remained still. Rizzoli tests the image as he moves from side to side then bends over looking up. The image reflects none of these movements. *It's mythic so unreal from the start, product of some ancient's storyteller's imagination. Then, reproduced with variations of look — sculpted, painted, photographed and e-mailed, you name it. Somehow this image got stuck to my mirror. Internet age is all image.*

Rizzoli studies it. Not taller than me as I first thought, Rizzoli thinks, realizing it's about his same height, girth and weight as himself. *Our waists are about level. Comparison ends there.*

Rizzoli can't take his eyes off the creature because the virtual looks so real by this time in the mirror. He watches its refection. The beast lifts its left leg. Rizzoli's own left leg lifts. *My left leg repeated that without my willing it.*

The creature's left leg lifts again and Rizzoli tries to make his leg stay unbent and keep his foot on the floor. Fighting a force to raise and bend it, Rizzoli is about to give up but then the force stops.

"Take that, goat-man."

With that, the beast steps out of the mirror in full three-dimensional form. Rizzoli darts back out of the way as it goes by into the living room, noiselessly! *Why aren't its hooves clattering on my wooden floors?*

Why? Instantly it comes to him. *Because it's still an image is why? Image of some other kind, I bet — hologram maybe.* Rizzoli goes near and slowly sweeps his arm through its chest. *Like air, nothing of him is solid. Yet, it is so life-like, no one else would know the difference. Like a figure from futuristic virtual reality.*

Rizzoli had his head down while pondering this and when he looks up the creature has vanished. *Gone for good? Invisible? Still here?* Rizzoli has no way of knowing. Rizzoli relaxes some but is now late for work.

Anyway good I'm rid of that creature's images. The room is silent. He squelches his urge to question this whole matter. *In this era, trying to find out why is too often impossible for me, a waste of energy. A satyr is what it is.*

Suddenly, he veers off to get a peach, from the blue bowlful on the countertop in the kitchenette. He's no desire to have one; he's already had breakfast. *I can't take the time to eat one; I need to get to work.* Intending to go to the door; he's immobile.

Looking down, he finds himself carefully looking over the red, orange and yellows of the fresh peaches. Taking time looking at each, he finally sees The One, full, juicy and reddish ripe. As he leans over, he realizes his initial urge has grown into a sudden, burning desire for this lush peach.

I'd never feel this way for a peach? It's not me doing this.

It's the Satyr doing this? He's possessed me – directing and... possibly feeding off my own sensual acts?

Yes. Rizzoli gently clasps the peach between both hands, deep cleft on the upside. It's delicate fuzz his fore finger begins softly stroking. The tip of his tongue, then, opens out the cleft before his forefingers press down slowly opening out the tight sides.

Rizzoli is surprised *this animal inside has me practicing being so gentle with the peach. Inhibiting its lust to be this gentle must be hard; is it trying to learn the modern art of seduction?*

Wait! Can the satyr still hold back? Rizzoli's tongue darts out breaking the peach's skin, penetrating deeper into the juicy pulp, giving off the scent of peach nectar and deeper still until juice swells up and runs down the over ripe fruit. He sucks and licks up the streams before his tongue is wildly pushing the flesh wider.

He hears salacious sounds. His ravenous mouth tastes peach. His tongue touches the hard pit as more juice flows down his lips and cheeks. *Is it practicing rape on… a peach??* His tongue penetrates even deeper into the juicy pulp, giving off the scent of peach nectar and deeper still until juice drips from the very ripe fruit.

Rizzoli is far from sated but, needing a moment to breath, he sets down this ravished fruit. Even with his senses still inflamed, he is startled at how he opened up the fruit (a flash memory has him seeing the start of some of his wild love sessions with his long-time woman Phoenicia. Now, weeks after they fought, she's still not talking to him and has rebuffed him time and again.)

I am horny; but nothing near the satyr's lust mid-way with this peach.

Now, remembering their fight, he abruptly turns away from the peach and strides back into the bedroom. Turning to the mirror, Rizzoli thinks he sees the Satyr's image for a split-second before it vanishes and his own reflection appears.

Hurriedly Rizzoli changes his shirt spotted with peach juice for another when it occurs to him, *the satyr knows no foreplay I bet; that's why, at first with the peach, he held back his lust and had me be so gentle with the peach. But midway, he had to lust.*

I bet the satyr is searching for a way to combine himself with a modern man who can start the lovemaking with a soft touch and enough foreplay to arouse some woman for the hidden beast's lust. Rizzoli thinks, *it's a possibility. May be long odds but who can know in dealing with... a Satyr?*

Rizzoli goes into his living room to find his cell phone. Where did he last put it down? On the couch he finds it.

(2)

Grapping his cell phone, he goes out the apartment door onto this topmost fifth floor landing, turns and starts down the many flights of stairs. He sees the halls are empty in his brown stone apartment building, by now others are out to work, wherever. Holding onto the handrail, he starts down the stairs. *Wait!*

He hears on each of the first stairs. A Clack, Clack, Clack. And looking down, he sees he's morphed into the satyr. *My shoes and socks gone and I share cloven hooves.* He feels the hair on his head. *What are these? Horns – on top of my head? My ears are pointed and soft inside. What has happened? Have I been swallowed whole inside this solid, real-life Satyr! Shit.*

Mythic creature turned real. Creature swallowed me up, a real Satyr encasing my naked body whole inside it. Making me take on its form. Not going off to work, like this, am I?

Rizzoli panics, feeling himself molded inside to the satyr's shape, just beneath its skin and hide. *Where did my clothes go? He disappeared them. Why? So my own bare flesh would be easier to form to its shape.*

Will I ever be me again, loosed from the beast? Again he feels his hair. No horns. What? "I could have sworn moments ago, I felt them." He says softly, in his own voice.

He tries to walk and struggles to balance upright on his new, hard goat feet. Slowly, he starts going down the other steps trying to go quietly—click, clack, click. It's difficult; he's managing it.

He tries to be stoical—*It is what it is. Suck it up,* he tells himself, *When the going gets tough, the tough get going. Show the beast, you can take his best.*

On the fourth floor landing, he hears a sound below, peaks over the banister down to the second floor and sees coming, *Daphne from 4B, the apartment right behind me now. The beautiful Daphne is coming up.*

Son-of-a bitch! Satyr has just swallowed me. Dammit! In an instant he is terrified. *Daphne will see me as a wild beast No wait! She will see the balls out satyr but cannot know I am trapped inside it.*

His terror returns; he's light-headed. Such is his wariness of this unknown mutant animal, he fears, any second, the satyr will vanish and leave him, the same old Rizzoli standing here but naked, exposing myself to Daphne.

Worse even, the beast will leave me here visibly attached to its naked lower goat half and it will vanish invisibly attached to my stolen human lower half. Anxiously, Rizzoli awaits Daphne being suddenly confronted and terrified by the beast itself… or by a naked me… or by a half me welded to a half goat.

She's coming up nearer. What can I do? Don't say a word. If she hears my voice come out of goat-man, I don't know what she'll do. Wait! The satyr is still holding Rizzoli's cell phone. No Satyr has a cell. No way. Quickly, satyr-he sets it down on the floor.

Rizzoli-in-the-Satyr is ready to *head-on face Daphne*. He waits. Daphne comes into view more and more, higher and higher. Will the beast expose me?

With her back to the Satyr, she comes up the last steps. Daphne comes around the corner. Her head is down noticing the lost cell phone. Her hands are too full of grocery bags to stop to get it. She looks up and walks right through the two of them as if they weren't there. *How could that be?*

Satyr morphed him and me to be invisible. We each have the same form as if I am in the satyr's casing so Daphne can walk through us without knowing either one of us is here.

Daphne has walked on, set the groceries down, turns and is coming back. *WHY?*

WAIT! She walks through the two of them a second time, wanting to retrieve the lost cell phone. She bends over to get it. As she sits down on her spiked heels, her bare midriff shows in back. Her full ass and flush hips are enticing; the small of her back is bared. And, as she turns her head down to the phone, her black hair falls forward along the side of her face, revealing the nape of her neck. On bent knees, she stays examining the phone. Her long legs show.

Go near and excite her, Rizzoli tells himself, *you' re invisible, airy. She can't know you're here even. Wait a second.* Rizzoli has a hunch, *the satyr, letting me take the lead, wishes to see more about foreplay with a real woman...not a peach. ,*

Moving compellingly toward her back, Rizzoli catches the scent of her perfume and sees appear a "real" lone nose suspended *(... Mine? Has to be...I recognize it.)* in mid-air to take in her scent of lavender

Rizzoli's desire is now overwhelming to have his own tongue graze over the soft downy hairs on her neck. His tongue appears and lovingly does this. Daphne shudders with delight. The tiny hairs on her neck are like the earlier peach fuzz, huh?

His own mouth and lips appear around his tongue and instantly, he teasingly gives the softest, slightly moist kiss on the little hairs of her neck then lightly blows. *She must think it's the hallway breezes. She moans softly heard by his appearing ears.*

His right hand appears; its forefinger he puts in his mouth, lubricates and traces lightly around her ear then blows in it She shudders then reaches her hand around to find out what is arousing her. His hand disappears faster than she can ever know. She turns her head to see. His mouth, tongue, lips, nose, ears and hands disappear faster than her eyes can see.

She stands up, back to him still. She purposely lifts her hair up, off her neck. Rizzoli's lips reappear to lightly kiss her neck, again and again giving her a shiver.

Daphne turns and walks away, his cell phone in hand. She opens and closes her door. The second, she turned to go into her apartment, Rizzoli had seen his bodily hand, tongue, lips, mouth, nose and ears vanish back into the invisible. Rizzoli has a brief after -image of his tongue, lips and other sensory body parts alone, suspended, working away in an erotic dance to gently arouse the beautiful, voluptuous Daphne.

Go inside, be her particular phantom lover responding only to her own special desires, urgings, fantasies.

His mind voice has to be his own animal aroused by the satyr's, Rizzoli's is tempted to slip through her shut and locked door. *You're invisible. How would she know?*

Do it. Rizzoli. He is tempted but reluctant. Aroused himself; he fears what the satyr's lust might force him to do. He remains in place.

Because of his hesitation, Rizzoli's fears *the Satyr will retaliate in a rage, rush us inside invisibly, ravish Daphne, flee alone invisibly and leave the real, visible me inside, compromised, naked — a criminal soon to be imprisoned for sexual crimes. Sets me up to take the rap for him. My only defense, "Judge none of this was my doing..."*

Now, turning opposite her apartment, he's stunned to see the unseen satyr first emerge a hologram, then morph to the mirror-like image, *Has the beast been studiously watching at the end of the hall?* Then it vanishes with the hint of a smile.

Wait! Maybe, back upon first going out the door, the satyr's seamlessly solid hologram encased me — never a real satyr. I was inside the creature's image. The hologram was so solidly life-like coming down the stairs no one could've seen I was inside the satyr's three -dimensional image.

It seems a taboo for it to turn from image to being real in the modern world. Remaining some type of image seems sacred to this satyr, for some reason. I think even when invisible, it retains an unseen ghostly image.

My believing it was real was due to my being so terrified at first, I had hallucinated feeling true horns on my head and hearing the "Clack, Clack" of real hooves on the stairs.

Recalling the instant the Satyr vanished, Rizzoli remembered, *he gave the hint of a smile. What kind of smile? Satisfied?*

Rizzoli glances down to see he's back in his normal clothes in the hallway. He's delighted at this return to his normal self.

Hurriedly, Rizzoli goes down the next flight of stairs to the floor below, when it occurs to him, *Wait, if the Satyr had me inside, both of us invisible, why did it use, not his own, but all my sensory organs — hands, nose, tongue, and all — to arouse Daphne? Sure, to observe foreplay with a real woman.*

But, remaining only an image, maybe it also used me as a host from whom to absorb my piecemeal sensory experiences like touch with my hands, mouth and so on.

In fact, as an image alone, it was limited only to virtual physicality but discovering a host changed this, thus, the happy satyr, smiling.

Before discovering and testing a host, this satyr, without sensory feedback, could read and urge a woman's ongoing erotic fantasy unerringly to a peak orgasm. But, it got only a voyeur's satisfaction, not "hands on."

After the satyr has stayed away for a good time, Rizzoli is overcome with a terror of the unknown — *if or when the beast will take me over again. If so, Where? At work, no not there, please. Will he make himself into a light hologram image of a satyr, with me a naked captive inside, visible to the passing pedestrians — me, real, itself a mere image of the real.*

Or, forgetting this, Rizzoli gets anxious that the satyr's lust *will get me so aroused that the animal will have me invisibly use my real sensory organs to mistreat a woman — a thing I would never do of my own will.*

When Rizzoli calms himself down and is thinking clearly, he has hope, *none of this will happen in public at least. My hunch (… probably a rationalization on my part…) says this satyr is forbidden to make himself or anyone else a public spectacle.*

What I think is the creature is on a visit here from a living parallel world of myth and to warrant this chance must heed a few strict rules — like remain an image with the moderns. If he does not, he can never go back to its home.

Putting it this way, Rizzoli gets some needed relief from worry. *Even if I know I'm wildly speculating.*

(3)

Wednesday afternoon.

Only minutes before, on the 59th Street Subway platform, the Satyr invisibly had come behind Rizzoli, disappeared him and transported them both here to some corporation's executive meeting room, many floors up in a midtown office building.

Now, as the presence inside the phantom, Rizzoli stands in back of a seeming beautiful woman with short black hair, white silk blouse and navy blue suit with a short skirt. She is sitting at the head of a long polished table, and the other board members sitting, are all men in expensive suits.

Move to the side. Get a better view of her. Rizzoli does. Instantly, he recognizes, *Collette. Collette.* The power partner of his French clients, he'd taken her to lunch just a few weeks ago. Then, he saw her as very sensual and alluring. *She is magnificent. She is smart and strong but also soft and voluptuous.*

Invisible, you best ease yourself under the table near her. He does. Her legs are showing, with her navy blue hose stopping at mid thigh, then her flesh. Sensing the contagion from the beast's lust, Rizzoli suddenly is very aroused and desirous. He reminds himself the Satyr made this circumstance and it's for foreplay—. so, I'm guiding him in this although likely he has to feel he's still fully in charge.

Nothing forced. For all has to be natural. I'll read her natural desires. Her natural desires you follow, yes. Rizzoli's nose and two ears appear in mid-air.

Above, in the meeting, Rizzoli realizes Collette, as top executive, has asked the whole board a question he didn't hear fully, requesting each one"…to give your thinking on the best market for our new perfume, "Erotica" the scent I've on right now. It's divine."(…*It is*…)The room goes quiet as she gives time for all to prepare their remarks.

Suspended before him in midair, Rizzoli suddenly sees — his nose and half-listening ears—his hands. Moving these between her slightly spread legs, his fingers begin stroking gently, smoothly, her inner thighs past the stocking to bare skin on her left leg. Her legs shift easing slightly apart; *she got a tingling sensation. I know.*

Rizzoli sees his hand, ears and nose vanish before she can see them as she takes a glance under the table to check on the nature of her agitation. Nothing there, she seems to decide. She edges her chair closer to the table. Rizzoli's nose, hands and ears again appear hanging in air. After again stroking her upper thighs, his hands press outward gently. She opens her legs slightly more. Her private scent comes to him. *Divine, too.*

"Yes, Warren," Collette asks, "What can you tell us?" As he answers, "Since our new perfume's test market was specifically Provence then I think..." Rizzoli takes in a deep scent of the perfume. Now appearing along with the other sensory organs are his mouth, lips and tongue. *Let her rare scent intoxicate. Yes! Yes!* Rizzoli tries to hold back becoming delirious with desire.

Give her the sensations again: inner thighs gently stroked, legs slowly parted. Then, kiss. Upward past the stockings and bare skin on both her thighs, his hands press outward gently. She parts her legs. Her cleft invites inside mounded dark blue panties. Rizzoli gives her mound a long, soft kiss. He feels her legs quiver.

As another executive begins, "Setting aside for the moment our test market being as stated, I think..." Rizzoli imagines Collette hasn't heard a word, as she is trying to detour her own erotic fantasy and its sensations engulfing her. *"Never before have I been so overcome with... "* He intuits her mind voice saying.

"Gentlemen, stop for the moment. I have something urgent I just remembered." She stands up from her chair. The Satyr-Rizzoli leaves from under the table. The two follow her as she exits into the hallway and enters her private executive restroom. The paired male, possible lovers follow closely beside her. The door locks behind the three. The invisible Satyr and Rizzoli stand waiting.

She sits in the sofa chair, slides down, pulls her skirt up and slips off her panties. *She's waiting to see what will happen, how much farther her erotic desire will take her.. Let her anticipation build. Let her wait expectantly. Not yet.*

Her head goes back, eyes closed. Legs part and rise up to rest on the soft arms of the chair; she's opened and waiting. *Ravish me, her mind urges.* Being her primary lover, the host, with the vital flesh, sees appear his own real prick, hard and afloat in the air. Her eyes she has closed, now even tighter in anticipation of a special something.

Now, yes. Rizzoli wants her to imagine she is being ravished as she had only just dreamed. Her dream is his own vision, specially guided by the satyr.

Rizzoli penetrates her hard and deep; knowing the satyr's image is channeling every sensation of this. Her body responds in kind thrusting, twisting, the three are as one and go on for a long, long ecstatic time before a calm comes.

Know that none of my past lovers had ever shown me the heights of my unspeakable desires. (Reading her after-thoughts.)

Rizzoli is confused but grateful: *All of this can only have resulted from the combined secret sharing of satyr and a modern male adept.*

Now the Satyr/ Rizzoli is pulling away. She senses the powerful something leaving. She begs it not to go, then to return, soon, anytime. The Satyr/Rizzoli stops and waits near the sofa chair, satyr's image shows in the round gold mirror over the sink. Rizzoli is spent and stunned to see this image. *Won't she see it?*

Having gathered herself together, she moves out of the chair. Before the same mirror, she redoes her make-up, puts her loose hair back in place. *Only I see its image.*

Then, she goes out the door and down the carpeted hall to return to her proper place in the boardroom. The Satyr/Rizzoli overhears her say, "Sorry, go on with the test market report" as they move past the door to the elevator.

Outside, the Satyr disengages from him. Rizzoli materializes out of nowhere as the normal Rizzoli. The satyr stands in a ghostly image unseen to all but Rizzoli who is wondering *Who knows what normal is…in this global virtual reality era? The Satyr now is invisible but seems here still.*

Pondering this new "normal." Rizzoli wonders whether in *having their way with Collette — satyr's image and especially me, the physical host — did we in some way rape her without her knowledge or consent?"*

"No, her own actions signaled her consent and always being conscious of her doings. She was able to stop it at anytime."

" Besides, with all of her lover invisible, she could not perceive this as more than her own erotic fantasy." *She initiated her uniquely personal erotic fantasy of an ideal phantom lover that brought her to her dreamed of orgasm.*

Never seeing any of Rizzoli's physical hosting for the satyr's sensory organs, she felt all of this fantasy loving to be just as real, as the satyr's image did in its own, different way.

" All right. A plan is combine the modern and the mythic with the aim being to go on to satisfy deserving women. With soft touches you provide the foreplay and when she is aroused, then you respond to the big burst of mythic physical lust that brings the high arousal you need to bring the woman fullest satisfaction.

Rizzoli listens, curious that: *while I'm the opening act the proud satyr claims to start the finishing lust of the host. Is the satyr being sly and conning me with this talk?*

"I'll have to think about all of this." Rizzoli says. "You've given your aim. I need to weigh matters...since there is no modern legal precedent for consent in such unusual circumstances, it seems a matter of individual conscience"

"Conscience. What's that?

" Nothing to you. "

So my mythical self, absorbing you, means there are no modern laws for crimes applying to our twosome. So, as long as this lasts, we two ought to dedicate ourselves to getting and giving pleasure."

The satyr disappears before Rizzoli can follow up with more of his side of all this. He's left with matters just now boiling to the surface. *That satyr sex leaves me out of any real control — choice of a woman and where and how she's seduced — makes me furious. Even more, I hate the satyr for seeing me only for my piecemeal physical assets and making me a spare parts sex object and taken for granted. No more.*

Stunned and guilty for having gone along, he can't believe, *this beast, disappearing and reappearing me at will — without my consent. Listen, goat-man, from now on I reclaim my prick for my own use — not for sharing. I direct it with whom, where and how I choose.*

(4)

Friday, before midnight

The hologram Satyr having taken him over earlier this evening has now let Rizzoli loose in a big dance club somewhere in New York. The lights are dim; a strobe light revolves dots of light everywhere: on the walls, floor, ceiling, dancers, the bar and the band sending a loud pounding beat. Rizzoli is drunk but he has no memory of where or when he had his liquor before arriving here this instant.

A hundred and more women are dancing with one another in various groups large and small, dancing wildly. Everything keeps shifting shapes pulsing to the strobe's flicking light. The hour seems late. All have had plenty to drink. A few women dance with real abandon, bodies able to merge as one with the music, loosing themselves in sounds, swirling dots, sweat, heat, a derangement of all senses.

Strange. This is one club Rizzoli doesn't know but likes it instantly. Dressed in his favorite jeans with shirt out and good smooth-soled dancing shoes. Of those freely dancing, Rizzoli observes a few of their male dates.

Most are nearby—sitting or standing—most chatting techno-talk or working on smart phones.

The woman next to him wants to dance; his quick glance can tell. He turns; she smiles." Phoencia, Hello." How he's missed her. She puts her finger to her closed mouth, "Shhhhh. I love. No words. Let our dancing do the talking."

Dancing closely with a full-bodied, exotic looking lady like Phoenicia he instantly spots an approving glance from the satyr. *Don't you even think about it, Goat. She's mine alone, a grand love.*

Rizzoli dances with her even closer, intoxicated by the way she moves, eyes closed, letting the wild beat of the music move her body. *Yes!* His body moves with hers, both almost as one, merging their separate selves over to a single self. Yes! *As we did in years past until the fight.*

Across the way, Rizzoli sees the hologram Satyr, invisible and matching, fast, fluid moves with a woman dancing ecstatically. The Satyr nods to him and slightly smiles in his just learned to be cool way. Rizzoli nods back, with the exact cool smile.

Still dancing, Rizzoli later looks over at the many small café tables and he sees glasses of half filled wine rising up off tables to be grouped on a tray, hanging in air, and taken down a hallway as if by their own power.

The Satyr, invisible, is stealing people's drinks. Right in front of guys so immersed in techno talk, they don't register the magic of it.

Curious, Rizzoli returns his lady back to her table and drink, says he'll be back in a minute and goes down the hallway to see what's up with the Satyr. After turning a corner, he peers around the next one.

He catches a glimpse for the first time of the Satyr being real, bodily, in his own flesh, not an image or invisible and proceeding to down wine after wine. Almost all the glasses are empty,

Startled, he senses (...*if my earlier hunch was right...*) the drunken Satyr is on the way to breaking a forbidden taboo from his still existing home in the parallel world of the mythic—he can visit the modern but never be real here, especially in public.

Then he spots Rizzoli "My friend, my friend, Rizzoli who graced me with the gift of foreplay to use on these modern women before my lust (...*his lust absorbed from me...*)

"I need you to answer some questions for me."

Rizzoli says, "Sure", but requests this be quick since he wants to get back to his lady. "The love of my life, that lady", Rizzoli states in a firm way, looking right at the satyr's crazed eyes. "I can respect that, Rizzoli."

"But, tell me, friend, why is it these young men avoid at all costs dancing with the lovely wild ladies?

"Satyr, maybe these guys are self-conscious so when they dance, they think others are looking at them and judging how terribly they dance. So, their compensation is to be masters of technology."

" But now all are drunk. Drink dissolves that, no?"

"You think it would, but "the no dance" seems almost... is "in-built" the right word?"

"'Built-in, huh, even when drunk,"

"But, six or seven of these modern men and me," Rizzoli says, " are wildly dancing and love wine and women."

"I know, I see you drinking in the god of wine and dancing with her, my kind of lady." The Satyr's laughs but Rizzoli doesn't join in and says "She's my lady, don't forget."

"Kidding. I won't."

"So, most of them, are afraid of having to perform dance or sex with women, is that what you're saying?" The Satyr shakes his head in disbelief.

Rizzoli shrugs." Who can say for sure."

The Satyr returns to being invisible. He's still a shape-shifter, Rizzoli's thinks, *so could be he didn't break a taboo. Must be hard for him to feel he needs a modern host.*

But, right now, drunken, riotous merriment is the mood of the Satyr as the two go back to the dance floor. Watching the satyr weave through the crowd of standing men and start dancing out amidst the swirling women, Rizzoli realiz-es how very drunk the satyr is on all that wine—*the fruit of the great god Dionysius, his hero.*

Rizzoli takes up with his Phoenicia again and goes out on the dance floor. The band is playing a slow tempo number. Each moves tight to the other. She begins tonguing his ear. Adoring her in this moment, and she him in this moment, all is right.

Phoenicia is, as the Satyr claimed earlier in the back room, "the real thing" one of those smart modern women who still has the most powerful link to the god of the vine Dionysius, who brings joy, ecstasy, and beyond that, the extreme.

Suddenly, Rizzoli hears the " Clack! Clack!" sound of cloven hooves mingling with the loud noises. Down amidst all the moving women's heels Rizzoli glimpses a pair of flashing, hooves, *the satyr's, yes, fleshed out,* **real**. No one stops to notice. Otherwise he is keeping himself invisible.

Rizzoli takes Phoenicia to the edge of the floor. Chancing it, he tells her of the mythic Satyr's visitation to this modern day and his morphing ability. She is not surprised in the least; instead laughs. Pointing out the hooves, the two watch. The hooves begin dancing wildly.

Suddenly above his hooves, Rizzoli sees appear the whole of the satyr's real lower half body, nothing above it, top half not there (*must really be drunk, did he loose himself doing a half real, half invisible?*). Calves, thighs, butt, waist and member itself are real and moving, swaying and flopping to the beat.

In the near dark with dots of the strobe flowing over all, no one notices. In plain sight of all, his real animal half is dancing, the human half invisible, Yet, only he and Phoenicia seem to notice and begin laughing wildly and hugging.

They see the satyr's real top half body join with the lower before he maneuvers around behind a black eyed, black haired, beautiful woman, looking to be of an exotic mix of races. Clearly the unseen goat eyes, Rizzoli knows, have picked out a female pearl, one whose senses are momentarily dissolved into the ecstasy of movement.

The satyr's hands, Rizzoli now sees, slip around her and up underneath her loose fitting red top, cupping her bare breasts. She presses her backside into what Rizzoli knows she can only imagine is the phantom manhood of a longed for lover. Her whole body shudders in an instant. Her mouth opens in what has to be a sound of pleasure. She smiles at no one in particular and goes on dancing by herself, as the satyr moves aside.

Unwittingly, the Satyr is ecstatic—he has pleasured his and her animal selves.

Seeing Rizzoli, the satyr's real self instantly comes over and his voice says proudly. "Did you see me?" " Yes! Bravo!" The Satyr now claims he's proved he can show himself — "as real anywhere, any place in the modern world" — he claps his hands, in applause for himself.

"My own solo touch on her flesh was ecstasy. My own senses let me dispense with foreplay. Do it my way. Modern world is not wholly closed off to me." He pauses. "But don't worry, my friend Rizzoli. I could need you at certain times still."

" Need you still, for what, Rizzolli" asks Phoenicia, "What is he meaning?" Surprised, Rizzoli is at a sudden loss for words to explain the duo's exploits.

Then the Satyr moves aside and whispers something in her ear. Rizzoli's can't hear what but is sure the treacherous beast told her the whole story and about Rizzoli being host.

"No I don't believe you. I've the grand love and great sex, with you know who?" Rizzoli doesn't hear this, with loud music of the live band.

The Satyr turns ecstatic, hearing "great sex", he thinks it's him and motions to her.

"Never" Phoenicia rushes off insulted and, saying she's going to get a cab.

Rizzoli guesses Phoenicia feels that this has renewed her feelings of being estranged from him. Turning, he curses the satyr who is already scurrying away.

The real Rizzoli waves good-bye after her, he gathers himself together, and leaves anxious and sad — feeling not as drunk.

My fear of being left compromised by this satyr's lust has oddly just been proven.

(5)

Rizzoli returns to his brownstone apartment building at an earlier hour than he thought; his watch has near 2:00 A.M. Going up the first flight of stairs, he hears keys jingling, somebody getting the key for their door. Coming around the corner, he sees Daphne with her door half open, returning at the same hour

Always friendly to one another, Rizzoli is so glad he's now seeing her in normal circumstances, *compared to the last time.* The memory of that does arouse him again (*...only now I've got myself in control...*). Her special attraction for him was there even before the satyr. Yet he has never given her a hint.

"You are just the person I need to see. I think I found your cell phone. Did you loose it?" Rizzoli smiles, "Yes. I'm so glad it's not gone for good. I'm grateful, Daphne.."

"Listen I forgot where I put it for the moment but come on in, while I find it."

Rizzoli does. Daphne closes the door asks if he'd like a drink, while he waits, explaining finding it could take a while.

"Daphne, only if you share a drink with me."

"I will. I've vodka in the freezer. We each have a shot?" Rizzoli agrees.

She seems so natural. Before she always seemed slightly distant. *Natural, did I say? .*

Don't go there he tells himself.

She seems to be looking at him in an alluring way he's sure he's misinterpreting, *after my times with the Satyr. Not one of the women of wild abandon,* he thinks. *Is she?*

She suddenly says, "I need to tell you something. I've been attracted to you ever since I moved into this building but you didn't seem like the type would give me the time of day. "

He's astonished, "Truth is I'd never guessed that. I do have a desire for you."

She's astonished. "Wait one moment. I'll be back." She returns in baby doll black negligee and says, "Come in there. I can tell how many ways I've dreamt of you."

Rizzoli stands, hugs her. He can't believe what's happening with him and her. He feels lustful. *Remember foreplay. Follow her desires.* The two hug rapturously.

"Overthrow her desires; Take her." Rizzoli turns to see who it is. Across the room, he sees the full-bodied, flesh and blood Satyr has appeared suddenly here inside, frighteningly visible and very drunk. Rizzoli can see the leer in his eyes—*of course, the Satyr's first attraction to her came days ago in the hallway when she knelt to get the cell phone.*

"Daphne." Look out! An intruder has broken in here disguised in an old Halloween costume." She screams. " Run." Rizzoli warns, "Lock your self in the other room." She does.

Near by the kitchenette, Rizzoli grasps a long sharp knife.

"I take what I want!" The Satyr screeches. "I want her! She will be mine!"

"NO!" Rizzoli jabs at him with the knife. *Envies me.* Rizzoli realizes, the Satyr wants to ruin the Daphne I desire tonight for his own spite. This night has all gone to his head. Power hungry on wine, he's a tyrant of his own lust.

The Satyr hollers, "My willpower leads the way here"

"Never! NEVER! I'll kill you first now that you're real. Stab you from the out-side now that you're banished to being a modern mortal. GET OUT!" Rizzoli hollers. He moves toward him with the knife out. *Satyr can't take me over any more.*

"I've still the power to turn invisible," the beast boasts, as he backs up and shows fear.

"Maybe so but doing it," Rizzoli says, " takes you much time and taking over anyone is very difficult" Rizzoli had just thrown this remark out, guessing, but the satyr's jaw drops and his yellow eyes burn at Rizzoli.

Keeping him at bay, Rizzoli opens the door and backs the Satyr out until the creature turns and runs down the stairs.

Moments later, pistol shots ring out as Rizzoli hears, "STOP!" POLICE. STOP. More shots. Rizzoli runs down the stairs to the second floor landing and joins neighbors in pajamas looking out the window. Outside the front door, there by the huge blue garbage can for "RECYCLABLES," he sees the Satyr lying dead, blood flowing from different wounds.

Before he could turn invisible and escape, he ran into the police bullets, Rizzoli knows. *Real, no longer an image, he was dead with a bullet-riddled heart.* Sensing the satyr's mythic spirit vanishing—just one more death in the big city on Friday nights—Rizzoli feels elation and a kind of sadness.

Police sirens are sounding nearer. *Crossed worlds; Never was his world here.*

Walking back up the stairs, Rizzoli focuses on being back in his apartment. Closing his eyes he goes up, up and in, his door left unlocked.

Eyes closed, Rizzoli walks to a certain spot. He hesitates to open his eyes before his mirror. He does and is seeing, *myself? Is it? Yes; but; are my ears pointed?*

Epilogue

Saturday morning: 3:20 a.m.

Right then on his smart phone in a flash breaking news item Rizzoli glances over a story stating that police, acting in self defense, shot and killed a giant Satyr who had repeatedly threatened them with thrusts of a butcher knife.

A woman in the building told police, all she remembered was when "the creature appeared out of thin air" in her apartment, "she was alone and screamed, and soon saw a lone butcher knife chasing the creature—a knife-wielding phantom hero running after the intruder."

You saw me with the knife, Daphne. He wonders, if she might be protecting him from the police. Or, did the Satyr morph **me** to invisible last night?

Somewhere going down the stairs," she said, "the Satyr must have taken the sharp knife away from my phantom hero."

Hero. Rizzoli wonders, Daphne wasn't I your hero? Whose word is valid here? Mine. He thinks of going public with his version but decides to await any further developments.

But, unbeknownst to Rizzoli, Daphne having used the word "phantom" connotes to other women, a male lover, invisible was with her, too.

∅

Saturday morning: 9:i5 a.m.

Rizzoli notes social media are buzzing with millions of postings as this news has gone "viral". Rizzoli scans the wrap-ups for the most important items. By inference, he now becomes aware (before the satyr showed on his own mirror) of prior reports of women having "phantom lover" sex in New York City.

For instance, a few weeks before the satyr appeared to Rizzoli, the media had begun buzzing about a few select women in New York City, who revealed having had "nearly real" sex involuntarily with an invisible phantom male lover who appeared to act out their own widely different, deeply private, erotic desires in a dream.

"A total surprise. Amazing to me," said a 38-year-old widow from the upper West Side on a blog post. "This phantom released in me a deeply personal fantasy with the erotic sequence tailor-made to bring me to a peak orgasm, at least five minutes long. Men in their youth have no idea of a woman's needs. Instead, unlike the phantom, they always want you to act out their guy fantasies."

A 25-year old woman from The Village posted, "It's so rare to find a real male who is not too stressed or overworked 24/7 to go to bed with you. Too, an invisible lover is far better than the usual fumbling one, or the dud or the drunk. Or, the guy who wants you " to act just like his favorite porno star."

In those few weeks before the satyr landed with me, thinks Rizzoli, the creature satisfied women but had no modern male host, like me, who lent him **real** physical sensation throughout, starting with his learned foreplay onto his first feel of a real modern prick.

Now the wrap up tells of a women CEO of an international firm reporting a ladies room encounter with "an invisible thriller" that proved "the best sex of my life." Colette? For certain it's her — she gives no name. But Rizzoli knows.

As he continues, he senses the animal Satyr and the human phantom lover have merged together in the mass mind of the cyber world enticing women as yet untouched by the phenomenon and threatening men. Rizzoli reads from a different wave of postings:

These tell of males sitting with automatic pistols, like Glocks, guarding their sleeping women, waiting for "any lustful ghost" to show in their bedroom. Rizzoli laughs, imagining all the anxious men, armed and dangerous, waiting as dream catchers. He decides not to go public with his information.

The social media frenzy soon led to a flood of new ads and products, for example for new perfumes called: "Venus Sleep." "Virgin Nymph"

This along with further flurries of rumors of unbelievable sex with unbidden unseen lovers caused a nationwide frenzy. "Invisible Thrillers & The Erotic Frenzy of Women Nationwide"

Commentators told countless times of an ideal unseen lover coming to eager females of all ages throughout the country. Some commentators called it "mass hysteria." Women, not visited, envied those who claimed to be of the chosen. So, countless many began to lie about encounters to prove their attractiveness.

"Sleeping Women Run Wild" read many headlines.

Males were furious that a mere phantom could prove them so inadequate. So, a number of men started to accuse their women of luring the unseen lover in the first place. The women grew afraid and responded by never mentioning this ever again. News reports dwindled to almost nothing

It still goes on. Rizzoli knows, as a myth cannot be shot. He tells no one as the image of satyrs — he can't tell if it's the same one exactly — appear regularly on his mirror but are fearful of him being a past, tragic host and soon disappear and find other hosts to become maximum phantom lovers for a woman. He guesses on my mirror a new mythic visitor makes a first image and this is now a set ritual for these new coming satyrs. Then each vanishes. The rest is myth.

Water Seeks Its Own Level

Rizzoli hears that noise again, thinks it is from the water pipes inside the walls of his apartment building and, instead, finds, when he slides back the shower curtain...*a mermaid* ...in his bathtub.

In momentary silence, he stares. His eyes lock on hers; suddenly flashing a hesitant fear. *Who am I? Will I harm her? Sure she doesn't know.* He doesn't want to frighten her more; she's already been flopping agitated, helpless there. A slap! Of the tub comes from the fin of her fish lower half body.

"Easy," he says soothingly, so caught up reacting in this moment, he hasn't registered fully — *it's a mermaid.*

Where the mottled green fish half body ends at her narrow waist, he sees, from the last scales up, her smooth skin flow to bare breasts. She has long slender arms and an oval face framed with twisting, tumbling curls of dark brown hair. *Like the Venus of Botticelli but dark*, he thinks, *and a water creature.*

Gills. He finds himself looking for her gills. She must have some to immerse in water. He's glancing; she has none. Having forgotten himself, he realizes his once-over glimpse to discover her gills has caused her more agitated suspicion.

She flops. Tears at her hair. She speaks suddenly in wails, "Air here on land! I am drowning in it! Understand, can't you understand me?"

"Understand?" *If only I could.* "I'm trying my best."

"Trying is not enough! I am dying right now, do something."

"What? What do I do?

"What? I beg you, I need to go back in the sea. I only can live there." Her chest heaves from her deep breathing. Gasping louder now, she raises her voice, "I am begging, begging you, to take me back, back to the sea!"

Rizzoli fears for her. "You must have gills? Do you? Without them, won't you drown in the sea?" He pauses. "You have just lungs? Am I correct?"

" Yes. You saw through me. Yes. I am a freak! Kill me now, I beg you," she hollers, running her fingernails across her chest, leaving streaked, reddened marks. She's getting hysterical, it seems to Rizzoli. He's been at a loss with a few hysterical women in past situations in his life. He wants so much to cope well this time, do right by her.

"Kill me!"

Kill… a mermaid? An image comes to his mind of a bludgeoned mermaid lying in pools of blood in his tub, him standing handcuffed and police officers asking him his reason for the murder.

"Kill a mermaid, no, I could never do it," he says. "You're one of the legendary maidens loved for your beauty by sailors for centuries."

"Listen up, guy," she says, suddenly cold-eyed "Don't you get mythic on me. Kill me now. Do what I say. You need me dead. Accept there's a larger explanation" Suddenly, she gives a hard study of him that instantly unnerves Rizzoli.

"Do it, hear."

He leaves the bathroom to gather his wits. *Get some perspective*, he tells himself. *Think of her as a phantom.* He gets ready to go back in, half expecting her not to be there. Surely she's a figure of his imagination. If she is there, he decides, the right inquiry is: Why me? Why my tub?

Stepping around the corner from his kitchenette back into the bathroom, he keeps his eyes closed. He counts, opens his eyes, instantly sees her, hesitates and asks, "Who are you? Why here?"

She starts sobbing and begins to tell a long halting story about her supposed pre-set purpose. She was to have been the one to migrate from water to land to start propagating a new, more intelligent species. She looks at him longingly, " after yours is gone."

Rizzoli is stunned. Gone? *Gone!*

"Just make love with me," the mermaid says, no longer sobbing.

What does she mean? She is solid fish from the waist on down to her flippers. More hopelessly, Rizzoli intuits, *Beautiful, beckoning mermaids symbolized heated desire, never fulfillment for the sailor. That's why these women had alluring breasts, faces, movements, but no sex organs.*

That this one thinks differently makes Rizzoli wonder if this mermaid in his tub is all there. *Could it be she is a little screwy in the head? Suicidal, yes. Yet, from the start she had to know her purpose was hopeless — since she's without reproductive parts.*

"No, forget love. Kill me. I can't exist in water … nor on land. Land is exhausting. Water used to buoy me up, never air. Land bruises. Life has no room for me, anywhere."

Rizzoli's heart goes out to her. Gently, he explains, "You, I, we all hope to be someone in time.…"

"Time? What is that?"

What is Time? "Time? Is nothing... but like you, we all want to be special. Few get this, so, if we accept that...,

"Few?" She is about to weep again. "I was deemed special."

Distractedly, Rizzoli goes on, " So, if we accept that, we can enjoy ordinary life."

"Ordinary life! Ordinary? My mission was: Be the perfect transition figure. I'm not!" She begins weeping again.

Oh, not the crying. " It's all right if you are not the 'perfect transition figure' now," he says softly.

"You. You can never understand."

"Forgive yourself, if you can, for not immediately starting a new species."

Wanting to lend her perspective, he asks, "You know that all takes time?

"Time?"

"Time." *I forgot, that word is outside her grasp. Not in her world?*

Seeing she is exhausted, Rizzoli explains he's going to take her to lie down and maybe sleep. He kneels, gets his hands under her, lifts her and walks to his bed and softly lies her down on his thick white comforter.

Her breast brushes his cheek. She looks up, *longingly?* *Yes.* Wait, he remembers an old, film noir, late night movie, *Murder with a Stranger. Is she a femme fatale setting me up to take the rap for a crime? No, can't be.*

Kneeling by the bed, where she lies, he sees her hands reach out and feels her palms cradle his face. She thrusts her breast up, softly smiling. Slowly he caresses it; her nipple becomes erect and he circles his tongue slowly around it. It rises hard.

Something squirts into his mouth. Before he can react, he's swallowed it.

"There! The baby will come!"

"To you?" He's happy for her.

"No. To you," she says.

"How?"

"Wait and you will, as a land person how do you say it? Will, will..."

"Go on, " Rizzoli says, "you are doing fine. Will, yes?"

"Will be. Be fragrant? Fragrant."

Pregnant! Me?

"Pregnant? Meaning you?" he prods.

"I don't know, but it's good to be with child, no?"

He nods, "Yes." *Does she know what she is saying? Is she lacking the words?* She smiles and kisses him. Hugging him to her breasts, she quickly falls asleep. Rizzoli ponders a while, concluding, *It's not words. She is still in her world.*

Yet he cherishes the experience and the joy it brought her...*and myself. Not that I could ever share it by telling anyone of the story of the beautiful, delusional mermaid in my apartment once upon a time.* He undresses and gets into bed. He moves his hand down her full hip, feeling the rough scales; his feet are touching her flipper fin at the end of the bed under the comforter. He falls asleep.

Opening his eyes at the morning light, he sees she is still sleeping. He hears the garbage trucks and the men clanging cans down in the street. He hopes the sounds don't wake her; he covers her ear with part of the blanket.

Lying on his side, he stares at her lovely sleeping face, framed by tendrils of curls. Quietly, muffling the sound, he clears his dry throat a number of times. Something wet and firm slips from his mouth and lies nestled in the fold of his pillow. *Am I seeing a mermaid, tiny as a goldfish?*

Reaching across, he softly strokes his lover's face. She awakens gently. Deep, brown eyes glisten as she gazes into his eyes, smiles, looks down to where he points. Her smile grows.

"Oh, my!" She cradles the infant mermaid in her palms. She looks closely and informs him, "This little one has both lungs and gills."

"Look," Rizzoli notices the little fin of lower body is split into two distinct legs with a hint of feet. Her look becomes pure joy. "Yes."

Fully confident, the mother starts to inform Rizzoli of what the little infant creature's next step must be. "This I can't do myself. I can't walk. You have to cradle this tiny one in your hands and then walk…"

"Me?" Rizzoli gets anxious and thinks, *what if I drop her?* "No," he says. "You cradle this little one, then I'll carry you both to, where?"

"No. It has to be you carrying him," she insists, still fawning over the child in her hands. She explains how and what he must do in her inexact, conflicted way. He can only hope he's pieced together correctly her odd phrases about "water top of sea's big rock" and "let's go in." He repeats to her what he believes he has to do. She nods. He hopes she's understood him; he's not certain.

"Will it be safe?" he asks. "So small?"

"This precious one is under a higher power."

What do I know? Rizzoli nods, smiling, not trusting what is and is not possible anymore. She very carefully hands the little one to him.

"It will only take a short time," he tells her.

"Time?"

He forgot about her and Time. "No problem. I'll be back shortly."

Carefully, he follows her instructions. He walks to the nearby shore, starts across the sand pocked with footsteps, stops, opens his cupped palms to make certain he still has the precious one. *It looks like a merman. Is there such a thing?* He doesn't know. It has grown slightly; its features are more distinct. *Muscles. No breasts. Little pud?*

He wades out knee-deep into the ocean, climbs up a rock and sees the still tidal pool at the top. There he lets the little creature slide off into the edge of the water. Rizzoli is now amazed at what he sees. *The creature is some sort of catalyst, with hidden forces streaming up from the deep dark swarming to it.*

Suddenly he feels like weeping *for all humanity.* He is moved to tears by the fate of the tiny creatures within the little pool soon to be swept out into the big, foaming sea with the next high tide.

After hurrying back to his building and up the stairs, Rizzoli enters his apartment, eager to greet his new beloved.

She is not in sight. He looks in the tub. *Empty*. Under the couch. *No*. The bed. *No*. Then he sees a paper on the table.

It's a note from her. He reads it:

My Dear Rizzoli,

Worry not about me. From atoms to atoms, said some wiser one of your kind. So, we are shape shifters all. Thus, I'm off where I belong.

The transition figure has been born. Mario Rizzoli, you were the pure Mother to the One starting the species to follow yours, a new species whose domain will widen to include all the world, for they will be able to live both on land and under the sea.

Ever,

Mother? Virgin? Mother.

ACKNOWLEDGEMENTS

My sincere thanks Bordighera Press, especially to Fred Gardaphé, and to Anthony Julian Tamburri and Paolo Giordano, and to the Virginia Center for the Creative Arts, where I drafted several of these pieces.

I am grateful to the following persons for encouraging my work: Canio Pavone, for his editorial and publishing guidance; George Leeson, Greg Sarris, Penny Wright, Jeanine Flaherty and the Monet Group: Anne Mollegen Smith and David Smith, John and Irene Kochevar, Julian Kagan and the late Phil Bauman. Thanks also to The New York Times for its May 11, 2007 article about the life of Giovanni Passanante and the dispute over the burial of his head, which inspired "The Head," and to Gail Pellett, who brought the news story to my attention.

Jane, my wife, is on a pedestal all her own in terms of my gratitude for our decades of love and of sharing a literary life together and in appreciation of her own outstanding achievements.

About the Author

Mark Ciabattari is the author of *Dreams of an Imaginary Author Named Rizzoli; The Literal Truth: Rizzoli Eats the Apple of Earthly Delights;* and *Clay Creatures*, which matches two stories — Ciabattari's "The Urn" and a new translation of Luigi Pirandello's "The Jar" by Maria Enrico.

Montana born and raised, Mark Ciabattari long resided in New York with his wife, Jane, and now lives near San Francisco.

VIA FOLIOS

A refereed book series dedicated to the culture of Italians and Italian Americans.

HELEN BAROLINI. *Visits.* Vol 113 Novel. $22

ERNESTO LIVORNI. *The Fathers' America.* Vol 112 Poetry. $18

MARIO B. MIGNONE. *The Story of My People.* Vol 111 Non-fiction. $17

GEORGE GUIDA. *The Sleeping Gulf.* Vol 110 Poetry. $14

JOEY NICOLETTI. *Reverse Graffiti.* Vol 109 Poetry. $14

GIOSE RIMANELLI. *Il mestiere del furbo.* Vol 108 Criticism. $20

LEWIS TURCO. *The Hero Enkido.* Vol 107 Poetry. $14

AL TACCONELLI. *Perhaps Fly.* Vol 106 Poetry. $14

RACHEL GUIDO DEVRIES. *A Woman Unknown in her Bones.* Vol 105 Poetry. $11

BERNARD BRUNO. *A Tear and a Tear in My Heart.* Vol 104 Non-fiction. $20

FELIX STEFANILE. *Songs of the Sparrow.* Vol 103 Poetry. $30

FRANK POLIZZI. *A New Life with Bianca.* Vol 102 Poetry. $10

GIL FAGIANI. *Stone Walls.* Vol 101 Poetry. $14

LOUISE DESALVO. *Casting Off.* Vol 100 Fiction. $22

MARY JO BONA. *I stop waiting for You.* Vol 99 Poetry. $12

RACHEL GUIDO DEVRIES. *Stati zitt, Josie.* Vol 98 Children's Literature. $8

GRACE CAVALIERI. *The Mandate of Heaven.* Vol 97 Poetry. $14

MARISA FRASCA. *Via incanto.* Vol 96 Poetry. $12

DOUGLAS GLADSTONE. *Carving a Niche for Himself.* Vol 95 History. $12

MARIA TERRONE. *Eye to Eye.* Vol 94 Poetry. $14

CONSTANCE SANCETTA. *Here in Cerchio* Vol 93 Local History. $15

MARIA MAZZIOTTI GILLAN. *Ancestors' Song* Vol 92 Poetry. $14

DARRELL FUSARO. *What if Godzilla Just Wanted a Hug?* Vol ? Essays. $TBA

MICHAEL PARENTI. *Waiting for Yesterday: Pages from a Street Kid's Life.* Vol 90 Memoir. $15

ANNIE LANZILOTTO, *Schistsong,* Vol. 89. Poetry, $15

EMANUEL DI PASQUALE, *Love Lines,* Vol. 88. Poetry, $10

CAROSONE & LOGIUDICE. *Our Naked Lives.* Vol 87 Essays. $15

JAMES PERICONI. *Strangers in a Strange Land: A Survey of Italian-Language American Books.* Vol. 86. Book History. $24

DANIELA GIOSEFFI, *Escaping La Vita Della Cucina,* Vol. 85. Essays & Creative Writing. $22

MARIA FAMÀ, *Mystics in the Family,* Vol. 84. Poetry, $10

ROSSANA DEL ZIO, *From Bread and Tomatoes to Zuppa di Pesce "Ciambotto",* Vol. 83. $15

LORENZO DELBOCA, *Polentoni,* Vol. 82. Italian Studies, $15

SAMUEL GHELLI, *A Reference Grammar,* Vol. 81. Italian Language. $36

ROSS TALARICO, *Sled Run,* Vol. 80. Fiction. $15

FRED MISURELLA, *Only Sons,* Vol. 79. Fiction. $14

FRANK LENTRICCHIA, *The Portable Lentricchia,* Vol. 78. Fiction. $16

RICHARD VETERE, *The Other Colors in a Snow Storm,* Vol. 77. Poetry. $10

GARIBALDI LAPOLLA, *Fire in the Flesh,* Vol. 76 Fiction & Criticism. $25

GEORGE GUIDA, *The Pope Stories,* Vol. 75 Prose. $15

ROBERT VISCUSI, *Ellis Island,* Vol. 74. Poetry. $28

ELENA GIANINI BELOTTI, *The Bitter Taste of Strangers Bread,* Vol. 73, Fiction, $24

PINO APRILE, *Terroni,* Vol. 72, Italian Studies, $20

EMANUEL DI PASQUALE, *Harvest,* Vol. 71, Poetry, $10

Bordighera Press is an imprint of Bordighera, Incorporated, an independently owned not-for-profit scholarly organization that has no legal affiliation with the University of Central Florida or with The John D. Calandra Italian American Institute, Queens College/CUNY.

ROBERT ZWEIG, *Return to Naples*, Vol. 70, Memoir, $16

AIROS & CAPPELLI, *Guido*, Vol. 69, Italian/American Studies, $12

FRED GARDAPHÉ, *Moustache Pete is Dead! Long Live Moustache Pete!*, Vol. 67, Literature/Oral History, $12

PAOLO RUFFILLI, *Dark Room/Camera oscura*, Vol. 66, Poetry, $11

HELEN BAROLINI, *Crossing the Alps*, Vol. 65, Fiction, $14

COSMO FERRARA, *Profiles of Italian Americans*, Vol. 64, Italian Americana, $16

GIL FAGIANI, *Chianti in Connecticut*, Vol. 63, Poetry, $10

BASSETTI & D'ACQUINO, *Italic Lessons*, Vol. 62, Italian/American Studies, $10

CAVALIERI & PASCARELLI, Eds., *The Poet's Cookbook*, Vol. 61, Poetry/Recipes, $12

EMANUEL DI PASQUALE, *Siciliana*, Vol. 60, Poetry, $8

NATALIA COSTA, Ed., *Bufalini*, Vol. 59, Poetry. $18.

RICHARD VETERE, *Baroque*, Vol. 58, Fiction. $18.

LEWIS TURCO, *La Famiglia/The Family*, Vol. 57, Memoir, $15

NICK JAMES MILETI, *The Unscrupulous*, Vol. 56, Humanities, $20

BASSETTI, ACCOLLA, D'AQUINO, *Italici: An Encounter with Piero Bassetti*, Vol. 55, Italian Studies, $8

GIOSE RIMANELLI, *The Three-legged One*, Vol. 54, Fiction, $15

CHARLES KLOPP, *Bele Antiche Stòrie*, Vol. 53, Criticism, $25

JOSEPH RICAPITO, *Second Wave*, Vol. 52, Poetry, $12

GARY MORMINO, *Italians in Florida*, Vol. 51, History, $15

GIANFRANCO ANGELUCCI, *Federico F.*, Vol. 50, Fiction, $15

ANTHONY VALERIO, *The Little Sailor*, Vol. 49, Memoir, $9

ROSS TALARICO, *The Reptilian Interludes*, Vol. 48, Poetry, $15

RACHEL GUIDO DE VRIES, *Teeny Tiny Tino's Fishing Story*, Vol. 47, Children's Literature, $6

EMANUEL DI PASQUALE, *Writing Anew*, Vol. 46, Poetry, $15

MARIA FAMÀ, *Looking For Cover*, Vol. 45, Poetry, $12

ANTHONY VALERIO, *Toni Cade Bambara's One Sicilian Night*, Vol. 44, Poetry, $10

EMANUEL CARNEVALI, Dennis Barone, Ed., *Furnished Rooms*, Vol. 43, Poetry, $14

BRENT ADKINS, et al., Ed., *Shifting Borders, Negotiating Places*, Vol. 42, Proceedings, $18

GEORGE GUIDA, *Low Italian*, Vol. 41, Poetry, $11

GARDAPHÈ, GIORDANO, TAMBURRI, *Introducing Italian Americana*, Vol. 40, Italian/American Studies, $10

DANIELA GIOSEFFI, *Blood Autumn/Autunno di sangue*, Vol. 39, Poetry, $15/$25

FRED MISURELLA, *Lies to Live by*, Vol. 38, Stories, $15

STEVEN BELLUSCIO, *Constructing a Bibliography*, Vol. 37, Italian Americana, $15

ANTHONY JULIAN TAMBURRI, Ed., *Italian Cultural Studies 2002*, Vol. 36, Essays, $18

BEA TUSIANI, *con amore*, Vol. 35, Memoir, $19

FLAVIA BRIZIO-SKOV, Ed., *Reconstructing Societies in the Aftermath of War*, Vol. 34, History, $30

TAMBURRI, et al., Eds., *Italian Cultural Studies 2001*, Vol. 33, Essays, $18

ELIZABETH G. MESSINA, Ed., *In Our Own Voices*, Vol. 32, Italian/American Studies, $25

STANISLAO G. PUGLIESE, *Desperate Inscriptions*, Vol. 31, History, $12

HOSTERT & TAMBURRI, Eds., *Screening Ethnicity*, Vol. 30, Italian/American Culture, $25

G. PARATI & B. LAWTON, Eds., *Italian Cultural Studies*, Vol. 29, Essays, $18

HELEN BAROLINI, *More Italian Hours*, Vol. 28, Fiction, $16

FRANCO NASI, Ed., *Intorno alla Via Emilia*, Vol. 27, Culture, $16

ARTHUR L. CLEMENTS, *The Book of Madness & Love*, Vol. 26, Poetry, $10

JOHN CASEY, et al., *Imagining Humanity*, Vol. 25, Interdisciplinary Studies, $18

ROBERT LIMA, *Sardinia/Sardegna*, Vol. 24, Poetry, $10

DANIELA GIOSEFFI, *Going On*, Vol. 23, Poetry, $10

ROSS TALARICO, *The Journey Home*, Vol. 22, Poetry, $12

EMANUEL DI PASQUALE, *The Silver Lake Love Poems*, Vol. 21, Poetry, $7

JOSEPH TUSIANI, *Ethnicity*, Vol. 20, Poetry, $12

JENNIFER LAGIER, *Second Class Citizen*, Vol. 19, Poetry, $8

FELIX STEFANILE, *The Country of Absence*, Vol. 18, Poetry, $9

PHILIP CANNISTRARO, *Blackshirts*, Vol. 17, History, $12

LUIGI RUSTICHELLI, Ed., *Seminario sul racconto*, Vol. 16, Narrative, $10

LEWIS TURCO, *Shaking the Family Tree*, Vol. 15, Memoirs, $9

LUIGI RUSTICHELLI, Ed., *Seminario sulla drammaturgia*, Vol. 14, Theater/Essays, $10

FRED GARDAPHÈ, *Moustache Pete is Dead! Long Live Moustache Pete!*, Vol. 13, Oral Literature, $10

JONE GAILLARD CORSI, *Il libretto d'autore*, 1860–1930, Vol. 12, Criticism, $17

HELEN BAROLINI, *Chiaroscuro: Essays of Identity*, Vol. 11, Essays, $15

PICARAZZI & FEINSTEIN, Eds., *An African Harlequin in Milan*, Vol. 10, Theater/Essays, $15

JOSEPH RICAPITO, *Florentine Streets & Other Poems*, Vol. 9, Poetry, $9

FRED MISURELLA, *Short Time*, Vol. 8, Novella, $7

NED CONDINI, *Quartettsatz*, Vol. 7, Poetry, $7

ANTHONY JULIAN TAMBURRI, Ed., *Fuori: Essays by Italian/American Lesbians and Gays*, Vol. 6, Essays, $10

ANTONIO GRAMSCI, P. Verdicchio, Trans. & Intro. , *The Southern Question*, Vol. 5, Social Criticism, $5

DANIELA GIOSEFFI, *Word Wounds & Water Flowers*, Vol. 4, Poetry, $8

WILEY FEINSTEIN, *Humility's Deceit: Calvino Reading Ariosto Reading Calvino*, Vol. 3, Criticism, $10

PAOLO A. GIORDANO, Ed., *Joseph Tusiani: Poet, Translator, Humanist*, Vol. 2, Criticism, $25

ROBERT VISCUSI, *Oration Upon the Most Recent Death of Christopher Columbus*, Vol. 1, Poetry, $3

www.ingramcontent.com/pod-product-compliance
Lightning Source LLC
Chambersburg PA
CBHW050902180626
46814CB00007B/2861